Ken Methold has been writing professionally since he left school, and full-time for the past forty-five years. Most of his more than one hundred published books have been educational texts for schools and colleges, especially in the field of English as a Second Language. However, he has also had six novels published by major commercial publishers, written extensively for radio and television, and contributed to many magazines and newspapers. He now concentrates on researching and writing about all aspects of life in Regency Britain, and reviews new books, both fiction and non-fiction, for *The Historical Fiction Review* and other specialist publications.

Ken was born and educated in the UK but lived in Asia for many years before migrating to Australia where he now lives with his ceramic-artist wife, Sheila.

Ken's first historical mystery was his critically acclaimed pastiche, *Sherlock Holmes in Australia—the Case of the Kidnapped Kanaka*. That story was set in late nineteenth century colonial, pre-federation Australia and the Islands of the South Pacific, but now Ken sets his mysteries in Regency England.

In Search of Jane Austen
An Investigation of a Life

Ken Methold

Dedication

This little book is dedicated to my ever-patient wife, Sheila, who put up with me for over a year while I lived, if only in my mind, in Regency England.

Author's Note

This is a work of fiction, of speculation. It makes no claims to be an academic work. I just wondered what people who would have known Jane might have said about her if asked. I'm grateful to Philip Catshill for his assistance with historical accuracy.

Ken Methold.
Kiama, Australia.

Chapter One

One late spring morning in 1818, Sarah Kedron took delivery of a letter from the Reverend James Stanier Clarke, Librarian, Carlton House, St James, London. The address was that of the London residence of the Prince Regent, The Prince of Wales, the eldest son and heir of the mentally ill King George III.

The contents of the letter surprised her. Revd J.S. Clarke was inviting her to call at her convenience at Carlton House to discuss a matter he described as 'pertaining to the literary history of the nation.'

Sarah had never met the Revd J.S. Clarke. She was also neither a scholar nor a university don; she was a former actress, now a successful playwright whose works had been performed at The Theatre Royal,

Drury Lane, London's premier drama theatre. She had no idea what the librarian could want from her. As the daughter of Matthew Kedron—the author of *Corruption Discovered* and the publisher of *The Informer*, the *Weekly Police News*, and the *Monthly Inquirer*—and an occasional book and theatre reviewer for the *Monthly Inquirer*, a highly regarded political and literary journal, Sarah presumed that the librarian thought she had an interest in the nation's literary history, and that she would be interested in something he wished to show her. Perhaps a recently discovered manuscript by a famous, long-dead author. Whatever the reason for the invitation, Carlton House had one of the finest libraries in the country, and an opportunity to visit it was not to be ignored lightly. However, she decided to discuss it with her father before responding.

That evening, therefore, over dinner with Matthew and his chief editor, James Brewster, who lived with them, she raised the subject. James was not only her father's most valued employee, he'd also become a family friend and frequently dined with them.

'Perhaps,' he said jokingly, 'he intends presenting you to the Prince Regent. He is more than likely to be an admirer of your plays. He is often at the theatre with his mistress of the day.'

'The lady in question,' Matthew said, 'is the Marchioness Lady Hertford, and may or may not be his mistress. She is well into her fifties. And the prince's health is hardly robust these days. Excesses of every kind have taken their toll. I think, therefore, that her attractions are probably more intellectual than anything. She is known to be a highly intelligent woman.'

'She is certainly believed to be a close friend,' James added, 'and highly influential at court.'

'That's all very interesting,' Sarah said, 'but it does not answer my question. Should I accept the invitation?'

'If it comes, even indirectly, from the Prince Regent,' James pointed out, 'it should be considered as a tactfully expressed royal command.'

'A good point, James,' Matthew agreed. 'And apart from that, Sarah, can you think of any reason why you should not go?'

'Not really. Though I have a lot on at present with my new play about to go into rehearsal. But I'm curious. If I don't go, I'll wonder for ever if I have missed out on something important, or at the very least, something interesting.'

'Then go,' her father said. 'Take the carriage and a footman to present your card. You don't want to stand at the front door waiting to be invited in by some minor flunky. Arrive in style.'

'Very well. I shall go tomorrow. If I'm not home for dinner,' she added with a laugh, 'send the Bow Street Runners to rescue me from the clutches of His Royal Highness.'

And thus, on the following day, at eleven in the morning, Sarah found herself in the library of Carlton House. The room itself was surprisingly cheerful with large windows opening out into a walled garden. The books were kept in floor-to-ceiling shelving which lined the room. As Sarah was shown in, the Revd J.S. Clarke appeared as if from nowhere and greeted her with a bow. A short, thin man in his fifties, he dressed gloomily in clerical black. He wore a pince-nez halfway down his nose and slightly pursed his thin lips. He struck Sarah as being the kind of clergyman whose favourite reading would be sermons against sin.

'I am greatly obliged to you, Miss Kedron, for your response to my invitation,' he said with a voice as thin as the rest of him. 'I hope you will not think I am wasting your time.'

'That is what I am here to establish, sir,' Sarah said with a smile.

'Quite. Shall we sit?' He indicated two chairs near the window. 'The weather is fine and reasonably warm, and the garden is a pleasure to look at.'

When they were both seated, Clarke said, 'I will come to the point. Your time is precious; I am sure. The subject of my concern is the author now known to be Jane Austen.'

'*Pride and Prejudice*,' Sarah said. 'A wonderful book. Unique really.'

'Quite. And of five other titles.'

Clarke picked up a piece of paper from the small table between the chairs, likely placed there in readiness for their meeting. The librarian had obviously been confident that she would call.

'In 1811, *Sense and Sensibility* was published with the authorship attributed anonymously to "By a Lady." A copy was sent to His Royal Highness by our usual bookseller. He presumably assumed that it would be welcomed as it was published by Thomas Egerton, who specialises in military history, one of His Highness's main interests.'

'Curious,' Sarah said, as much as for something to say as anything. 'Did Egerton usually publish fiction?'

'No. *Sense and Sensibility* in 1811, *Pride and Prejudice*, two years later, and then *Mansfield Park* the following year, are his only novels. At the time, the author was not known to be Miss Jane Austen.'

'Did the Prince Regent read them all?'

'I do not know. I know only that he definitely read *Pride and Prejudice* and enjoyed it greatly. Indeed, he was so impressed that he instructed me to inform the author through her publisher that he would not be displeased if she dedicated her next novel to him. As instructed, therefore, I approached Mr Egerton only to be informed that he had not been offered the next novel. Entitled *Emma,* it was to be published by Mr John Murray, one of our most prestigious publishing houses. You may not be aware of the fact,

Miss Kedron, but John Murray is the publisher of Lord Byron. It beggars belief, madam, but Miss Austen, as we now know her to be, not only insisted on remaining anonymous but also had to be persuaded by the publisher to dedicate the book to His Highness.'

He paused and picked up a copy of *Emma* from the little table. He opened it at the title page.

'May I read you the dedication?'

'Please do.'

Clarke read aloud the following: 'To His Royal Highness, The Prince Regent; this work is by His Royal Highness's permission, most respectfully dedicated by His Royal Highness's dutiful, and obedient humble servant. The Author.'

When he finished reading, he said, 'I cannot think of a less effusive dedication. It is almost as if it were written under duress.'

'Perhaps she felt it was,' Sarah said. 'What did His Highness think of it?'

'He was not impressed. And he felt especially insulted by the author insisting on remaining anonymous. It was if she did not want to be associated with him in any way.'

Sarah thought it highly likely that this was exactly what Miss Austen had felt. The Prince Regent was widely despised for his extravagance and debauchery. Tactfully ignoring the likely reason for Jane Austen's behaviour, she said, 'Anonymity is fairly common with the first book of a female author, and even the second, usually for social reasons; they do not want to risk being associated with a book that is badly reviewed or a failure in other ways. Neither do they wish to be thought to need money. However, I have to agree that to remain anonymous for so long is unusual, especially one so amazingly productive. Four novels in four years is a remarkable achievement.'

'What is even more remarkable—though perhaps inexplicable is a more exact word—is that Miss Austen rejected out of hand what could have been the invaluable patronage of His Highness. Had the dedication pleased him, I believe it is possible, even likely, that he would have offered to head the subscription list for her next novel. For obvious reasons, everyone who wished to be noticed as a supporter of His Highness's literary tastes would also have subscribed. The publication would have made a substantial profit even on its first printing.'

Sarah knew this would have been the case. Although subscription publishing was no longer as popular as it had been for the simple reason that it had become difficult to obtain sufficient subscribers to guarantee a publication against loss. Any title, on any subject, with the Prince Regent as the first subscriber could hardly fail.

'Did you have an opportunity to meet Miss Austen and explain to her the value of the Prince Regent's patronage?' she asked.

'We corresponded on the matter, and Mr Murray arranged a meeting at his office. I regret to say that Miss Austen did not favourably impress me. She expressed no interest in his Highness's high regard for her work and …' The librarian paused and paled at the recollection of the insult he felt he had personally suffered. 'And when I suggested that she might consider writing a novel based on my experiences as a court official, she was, well, frankly abrupt to the point of brusqueness. And then when I attempted to inquire what her plans were for future books, she simply shrugged and brought the meeting to an end. I did not enjoy a favourable impression of the lady.'

Replacing the copy of *Emma* on the table, he said, 'There are two further items I wish to bring to your attention. Last year, John Murray published two further novels, *Northanger Abbey* and *Persuasion*. They finally revealed the author to be Jane Austen. By then she was deceased. Attached to the novels was a brief biography of the author written by her brother, Henry Austen. In this, he has little to say about his sister's literary output. He contents himself by listing some titles without any comment and concerns himself almost wholly with such matters as her sweetness of character, her piety and how greatly she was loved and so on by her family. His only other reference to the works is to insist that they were of little importance to her and that she had no interest in any financial benefits to be enjoyed from their sales. He also insists that she had no interest in achieving fame of any kind and had demanded that her name should not be associated with any of her books during her lifetime.'

'Extraordinary.' Sarah slowly moved her head from side to side in surprise. Jane Austen seemed to have behaved like no author she had ever met or of whom she had heard. Invariably they all sought—usually unrealistically—a degree of fame and fortune.

The librarian continued. 'Miss Austen died in July last year and is interred in Winchester Cathedral. I am reliably informed that her gravestone makes no reference to her authorship. It is as if her family, for one reason or another, are determined to disassociate themselves from her writing.'

Sarah fell silent for a few moments while she considered this. Then she asked, 'Do you have a possible explanation?'

Clarke nodded. 'Lady Hertford, who is a great reader of novels of all kinds, is of the opinion that the novels attributed to Miss Austen may not have all been written by her. Lady Hertford is especially adamant that *Pride and Prejudice* and, perhaps, *Sense and Sensibility* were not written by the same person as the other four books.'

'Goodness!' Sarah exclaimed. 'That is a most serious allegation. Apart from possible legal implications, there are other issues.'

'Precisely.'

'You are suggesting, if I understand you correctly, sir, that Miss Austen and her family possess information about her writing that she—and they—wished to conceal.'

'I can think of no other explanation.'

Sarah remained silent for a moment or two. Then she said, 'I am not at all sure what I should or could do about such a situation if, indeed, it exists.'

'You contribute articles to *The Informer*, of which I understand your father is the proprietor. Perhaps you could raise the matter in an article.'

'I would need a great deal more evidence before I could even consider writing about Miss Austen's possible plagiarism or worse,' Sarah said. '*The Informer* is not a scandal sheet.'

'I appreciate your hesitation, Miss Kedron, and it is one of the reasons I have approached you instead of—shall we say—the editor of *The Gentleman's Magazine*. I understand from Lady Hertford that his Royal Highness would like the matter to be thoroughly investigated. They are both of the opinion that the first two published novels and *Emma*, are of such quality that they may well become increasingly popular, perhaps even classics of their kind and as widely regarded as the works of Mr Samuel Richardson or Miss Maria Edgeworth. They think it important that the correct authorship should be attributed to them.'

Clarke stood up. 'Miss Kedron, I am most obliged to you for coming here today and listening to what I have to say. The matter is now in your hands to pursue or not as you consider appropriate.'

Sarah also rose. She offered Clarke her hand which he somewhat gingerly took as if he expected it to lead him into all kinds of debauchery.

'I will discuss everything you have told me with my father.' She inclined her head slightly. 'Good day, sir.'

Clarke bowed, and Sarah left Carlton House for home, deeply concerned by what she had been told. If, she thought, Jane Austen was not the author of the six books in question, especially of the brilliant *Pride and Prejudice*, then why had the real author allowed the book to be appropriated by another person? Such a mystery, she thought, might be worth trying to solve.

Chapter Two

Sarah's carriage waited to take her home, but she told the groom to go to Chancery Lane instead. As it was almost midday, Sarah supposed that her father might be lunching with James at their favourite chophouse, an establishment that not only provided the best meat but also the most up-to-date legal and financial gossip. Once there, she sent the carriage back to its mews stabling behind their home and office.

In anticipation that she would want to give them a detailed account of her visit to Carlton House, her father had saved her a place at their table. He raised a hand in greeting as she hurried across the crowded, noisy room to the alcove where they sat. As soon as she sat down, a pot boy rushed up with her personal pewter mug of ale. She thanked him and drank gratefully. Then she relaxed against the back of the tall chair.

'Well,' she exclaimed 'you will never guess what it was all about.'

'Did you meet the prince?'

'No, thankfully. Only his librarian. The Reverend James Stanier Clarke. A rather pompous self-important little man. He—or, if he is to be believed, the Prince Regent—is concerned that the six novels claimed to be authored by the late Miss Jane Austen may not actually have been written by her.'

'Bless my soul,' Matthew declared. 'What an extraordinary thing to summon you to Carlton House about.'

'There is more,' Sarah said and described the Reverend Clarke's other concerns: the author's reluctance to reveal her plans for future books or enhance her writing career with a novel based on his experiences as a court official. Sarah concluded by saying, 'It all adds up to nothing, of course. Yet the woman's behaviour is, at the very least, rather odd. As is her brother's.'

'Do you intend making any inquiries?' James asked. 'If you do, I can give you introductions to the publishers Thomas Egerton and John Murray. They are both anxious to be considered favourably by our literary editor. Hardly a week passes when we don't get at least one book from them for review.'

Matthew said, 'Surely there isn't really enough information about Miss Austen to justify your spending time on it.'

'You're right. There isn't,' Sarah agreed. 'And yet … well, let's just say that I'm intrigued. And it is probably a good time for *The Inquirer* to publish an article about her. She died only a few months ago and is buried in Winchester Cathedral. That in itself says something interesting about her.'

James nodded in agreement. 'From what I hear, she is certainly the most interesting of the women novelists.'

'Compared with *Pride and Prejudice*,' Sarah said, 'none of Miss Fanny Burney's or Miss Maria Edgeworth's novels stand a chance of being read in fifty, even twenty years' time. And as for Ann Radcliffe's gothic nonsense …!'

James said, 'Murray persuaded Sir Walter Scott to review Austen's *Emma*. Unfortunately, he was not wholly impressed by it.' With a cunning editor's smile, he added, 'How about a series of profiles, "Women Novelists at Work Today." We need to increase female readership of *The Informer*. And it's the women who buy or borrow all the fiction.'

Matthew nodded. 'That is an excellent suggestion, James. At present, our book review pages are rather lacking from a woman's point of view. What do you say, Sarah?'

Before Sarah could reply, a messenger hurried into the chophouse. He was one of several employed by the Drury Lane theatre. Looking around, he soon espied Sarah and hurried towards her. He handed her a sealed, folded note.

'For you, Miss Kedron. I am to await a reply.'

Sarah broke the seal and read the note. Her face clouded.

'There's a problem with my play,' she said. 'I must go to the theatre and find out what's wrong.'

To the messenger, she said, 'Tell the manager I'm on my way.'

The messenger hurried off, and Sarah stood. 'I'd better go now. I can't imagine what the problem is, but it's obviously something serious. We'll talk about this Austen business later.'

The Theatre Royal in Drury Lane was but a few minutes' walk from Chancery Lane. The manager, Samuel Arnold, looked up from his desk as Sarah entered and gave her an apologetic smile. Little more than a large cupboard, the office was so full of broken props, torn costumes, stained prompt copies and other theatrical detritus that it had the appearance of an unsuccessful pawn shop.

As Sarah took the only remaining seat, Arnold said, 'Let me say immediately, Miss Kedron, that in my opinion there is nothing wrong with your play, and I consider it an honour to be presenting it.'

From this statement, Sarah knew that a requirement to rewrite was in the offing.

'It's a little late in the day to ask for changes,' she said.

'I made exactly that point to Mr Kean.'

'Ah!' Sarah exclaimed. 'And what's his problem with the play?'

Edmund Kean, the current darling of the audience for drama, was the only actor who could fill the 3,060-seat theatre night after night. Well aware of this, he behaved disgracefully, often appearing drunk, or not appearing at all, or making frequent and unreasonable demands of the theatre's management. Under the terms of his contract, he held the right of veto for any new play that did not satisfy his ego.

'I regret to say, Miss Kedron, that Mr Kean does not think his role in your play is large enough for his talent. He demands another dramatic scene with at least one hundred lines.'

Sarah knew better than to argue that to include such a scene would destroy the carefully structured storyline and probably also the rhythm of the play. Such objections would be waved aside as being irrelevant. There was, however, just one good argument that might persuade Edmund Kean to be more reasonable. 'Surely he understands that if we make any changes to the play, it must be re-submitted to the Lord Chamberlain's office for approval before we can stage it. That could take weeks even if no changes are required.'

'I have explained that,' Samuel Arnold said, 'but Mr Kean is adamant. If necessary, the production must be rescheduled.'

This, Sarah accepted, was a euphemism for 'cancelled.' She also knew that her only hope of getting the play re-considered without delay by the Lord Chamberlain's office was to have a friend at court. She realised with some surprise that, only that morning, she might have met such a person!

'How long have we got?' she asked.

'I can extend the Shakespeare and put the Garrick play between it and yours. That could give us three weeks depending on the houses.'

If she got to work on the script immediately, Sarah could complete the rewrite in two or three days. That would give the censor two full weeks to do his worst. It should be enough. She was confident in her ability to avoid contentious areas.

'I will know by tomorrow if it can be done,' she said. 'I have an acquaintance at Carlton House who may be able to speed matters up.'

'That would be splendid,' Samuel Arnold said. 'I will tell Mr Kean how very accommodating you are being.' He stood up and bowed. 'I am really most obliged to you Miss Kedron. I hope to have good news soon.'

Sarah gave him a wry smile and left his office. After hailing a hackney outside the theatre, she instructed the driver to take her to Carlton House. If the librarian was there, she would find a way of enlisting his aid.

Chapter Three

The Reverend Clarke was surprised to see Sarah so soon after the morning's meeting, but he received her courteously, hoping for an advantage. He guessed that she would not have returned unless she needed his assistance in some way.

Always brisk and concise, Sarah came straight to the point of her visit. 'I have discussed the possibility of a long article in *The Inquirer* with my father and his editor, Mr Brewster, and they are both of the opinion that Miss Austen's life and works will be an appropriate subject for the periodical.'

Clarke's face brightened. 'Excellent. I am sure that will please his Royal Highness.'

'I would like to start making the necessary inquiries immediately. Mr Brewster will provide introductions to Miss Austen's publishers, and whatever they can tell me will be a useful beginning. However, I would not want to raise with them, certainly not at this stage, the possibility that Miss Austen was not the author of all the novels that now bear her name. I would need considerable evidence to support such a theory before I mentioned it.'

'I understand. I will inquire further of Lady Hertford.'

'Thank you. There is one other thing, Mr Clarke.' Succinctly, she explained the problem with her play. His response was better than she could have expected. He clearly wanted to be helpful and to demonstrate his influence at court.

'I am sure I can arrange for your revised play to—what shall I say—go to the top of the pile. I am occasionally asked to assist the Lord Chamberlain by considering matters in a new play that relate to the church. You will be aware, no doubt, that any statements favourable to Jacobite or popish interests have to be excised.'

'Of course.'

'When then may I expect the revised manuscript of your play?'

'Within three days.'

Sarah offered the clergyman her hand. 'I am deeply obliged to you, sir.'

'It is my pleasure to be of assistance, Miss Kedron.'

Sarah realised that sooner or later there would be a price to pay for his assistance, probably a request for an article to be published in *The Inquirer* about him and his work as the royal librarian. Perhaps even something flattering about the Prince Regent. Time would tell, but she need not presently consider the matter.

Feeling rather pleased with herself, Sarah decided to spend the rest of the day with Elizabeth Stockton, her artist friend who had a studio apartment in Cheyne Walk. An attractive possibility occurred to her. For the evening ahead, they could cross the river to Vauxhall Gardens where there would be music and dancing, and where they would encounter friends from their respective worlds with whom to enjoy the activities and refreshments that the Gardens had to offer. Tomorrow, she thought, would be soon enough to begin revising the play.

Elizabeth's maid escorted her up the five flights of stairs and opened the studio door for her. Her arrival caused Elizabeth's face to light up with pleasure. She hurried forward, and they embraced. Elizabeth was a little taller and considerably stouter than Sarah, and with her golden hair curled in a rope on top of her head, her appearance was in marked contrast to Sarah's, whose gipsy blood had given her almost jet-black hair and a slightly sallow skin.

'Dearest this is such a lovely surprise,' Elizabeth exclaimed. 'I wasn't expecting to see you until the end of the week.'

'I hope I'm not interrupting important work.'

'If only you were interrupting work of any kind! I am between portraits; the worst time for me. I cannot settle for anything. Your company is desperately needed.' Taking Sarah by the hand, she led her to a couch near the floor-to-ceiling window. 'Can you stay awhile?'

'Yes. And perhaps we will go to Vauxhall this evening. But before we make plans, I must tell you what has happened today. A most strange one.'

Over the two years that Sarah had known her, Elizabeth had become her closest friend. Although different in personality and temperament—Elizabeth was impulsive and out-going whereas Sarah was more considered and reserved—the two women were always completely at ease and secure with one another. Elizabeth, whose temperament was mercurial and who suffered greatly from her lack of confidence in her art, needed the emotional support that the far more self-confident and socially secure playwright was able to provide. Although only two years younger than Sarah, she was in many ways still more of a young girl than a mature woman. For her part, Sarah responded gladly to her friend's ebullience and treasured their friendship.

'Tell, dearest, tell all,' Elizabeth demanded. 'I so badly need cheering up today.'

'Well,' Sarah said, 'it all began with a summons to Carlton House.'

'The Prince Regent's residence! What did that old lecher want from you? Oh no! He hasn't designs on you as yet another mistress.'

'Nothing like that, thank goodness. Believe me, if I took a lover, he would not be so old and obese. No, it is all about the novelist, Jane Austen.' She related the events of the day in detail, and when she had finished and done her best to answer Elizabeth's many questions, she came to the main point of her visit.

'I think it is likely, my dear, that if I am going to write an article, I shall need to meet and talk to a lot of people. This means I shall have to travel, perhaps quite extensively. I was wondering if you would care to come with me—that is, if your painting commitments allowed you to.'

'Oh! Yes, yes!' Elizabeth exclaimed. 'There is nothing in the world I would like to do more. When do we begin? Do you have a plan?'

'Not yet. I expect that as I talk to people, the information I obtain from each will lead me to the next contact. I intend to begin with her publishers to establish a history of her novels. Who knows where that information may lead us? Our travel plans, therefore, must be flexible. I thought we might begin with a trip to Winchester. That is where she died, so we might be able to talk to her physician and friends in the city. Her tomb is in the vault beneath the north aisle of the cathedral. That in itself is a surprise. She was so little known during her lifetime as all her novels were published anonymously.'

'Why do you want to see her tomb?'

'I want to see what is written on her tombstone. I believe it will be not what one would expect.'

'When do you think I should be ready to leave here?'

'What do you say to Sunday?'

'Perfect. How long will we be away?'

'I don't know. We may come back to London from Winchester or travel elsewhere. Our journey will depend on what we discover there. Can you arrange for your maid to look after your studio and forward any letters and so on? We can always let her know our forwarding addresses.'

'That is easily done. Oh, Sarah, this is so exciting. And it is so lovely of you to ask me to join you.'

'There is no one else I could wish to ask.'

'Not James?'

'Ah, the dear James. No, he has work to do, but he is very enthusiastic about the project. As is my father.' A thought occurred. 'Oh, yes, don't give a thought to the expenses. This investigation is being paid for by *The Inquirer*.'

Tears of both happiness and relief appeared in Elizabeth's eyes. 'Your father is very generous.' She became thoughtful for a moment and then asked quietly, 'Does your father know that I am to be your travelling companion?'

Sarah laughed. 'Not yet. But he'll be delighted when I tell him you have agreed. I think his gesture will then be more of gratitude than generosity, dear. He would be greatly alarmed if he thought I intended travelling around the countryside on my own.'

She took hold of Elizabeth's hands and smiled conspiratorially. 'There is just one other thing. I shall explain to people my curiosity about Miss Austen by telling them that I am writing a series of articles for *The Informer* on women novelists. You, I suggest, I should introduce as the artist commissioned to provide appropriate illustrations for the articles. Houses and gardens. That sort of thing. Even line drawings of faces where relevant. Is that all right with you? It will be so helpful to have you with me during the interviews. Your thoughts on what is said—or left unsaid—will be invaluable.'

'It's a wonderful idea. I'll bring my smaller easel and water-colours. Oh, Sarah this is so exciting. I just know we'll have a lovely time travelling together.'

Sarah nodded and smiled. 'Of course, we will, dear. It was fun before, and it will be again.' She laughed. 'When we were trying to find out what had happened to Sir Charles Browning, we told people you were interested in ecclesiastical architecture. I don't remember anyone asking to see your drawings. Not one.'

'That was just as well. They are not my best, but I keep them as souvenirs,' Elizabeth said. 'They are very precious to me.'

Sarah stood. 'That is sweet of you. But now let us change our clothes and go to Vauxhall. We are sure to meet some friends there, dine and, perhaps, even dance a little. We'll celebrate the birth of another mystery to be solved. I'll call for you in an hour or so.'

The two women walked to the door where they embraced fondly.

Well-satisfied with developments, Sarah left to take a hackney back to Portman Place.

Chapter Four

James Brewster was as good as his word and, within an hour, had sent a letter introducing Sarah to Thomas Egerton at his bookshop and office at Charing Cross. Egerton had replied by return, expressing pleasure at an opportunity to meet the celebrated playwright and actress. The next morning, Sarah took a hackney to the Cross with high hopes of obtaining useful information.

Egerton had his desk at the back of the shop, presumably to keep an eye on his customers and observe how the two apprentices attended to their requirements. Recognising her as she entered—he was a frequent patron of the Theatre Royal—he stood up as an apprentice led her towards his desk.

'Miss Kedron to see you, sir.'

'Miss Kedron, this is an honour and a pleasure. Is there any chance of a repeat production of your splendid play *The Malevolent Mistress* this year?' He invited Sarah to be seated and signalled to the apprentice to bring tea.

'I doubt it, Mr Egerton, but there are plans for my new play to feature Mr Edmund Kean at Drury Lane. Much depends on the censor.'

'Ah, yes, that ridiculous office,' Egerton said as he resumed his seat. 'We used to be more fortunate than playwrights, but the situation is very different now. Although there is no system like the Lord Chamberlain's office by which we can have our books checked for sedition and goodness knows what else before publication, if after publication they are believed to contain matter that the government does not like, we can expect trouble. The newspapers and periodical press need to be especially careful. Your father must be very worried by the loss of press freedom.'

'It is a matter of grave concern to him, Mr Egerton,' Sarah said. 'The movements for reform in so many areas are stifled by the government's fear that the revolutionary spirit could spread from France to Britain. At least as a playwright, when my work has passed the censor, I need not worry about being arrested, unlike many of our political journalists who never know from one day to the next whether they will be arrested and tried on some ridiculous charge. There are government spies everywhere.'

Egerton nodded. 'Indeed, and I have no doubt that if Mary Wollstonecraft were alive and writing today, she would be languishing in prison. As would her husband, William Godwin. A good subject for a play another time? Perhaps for the American stage.'

Sarah allowed Egerton, who seemed a little nervous, to chatter on. He seemed a pleasant enough man, nondescript in appearance and a little pedantic, she thought, as a bookseller and publisher was often expected to be.

As the apprentice poured the tea, Egerton moved on from pleasantries to the point of Sarah's visit. 'I understand from Mr Brewster's note that you are interested in the life and works of the lady we now know to be the late Miss Jane Austen.'

'That is so. I would be most obliged, Mr Egerton, if you could tell me something about the publishing history of her novels.'

'I'll be happy to tell you about the three novels we published. I need to make it clear at the beginning, however, that my firm was not the ideal publisher for the lady. We do not usually publish fiction and have little experience in its sale.'

'May I ask why you made an exception for Miss Austen?'

'Of course. I was approached by one of my authors of military history to meet a friend of his, a Captain Henry Austen of the Oxford Militia. He was hoping to find a publisher for a book by a member of his family. I thought at first, he had written the book himself but lacked the confidence in it to admit the fact. The book was a novel, *Sense and Sensibility*. I pointed out to him that I knew little about fiction publishing, but he gave the impression of not wanting to spend time hawking the book around from publisher to publisher and was anxious to get it off his hands as quickly as possible.'

'I understand. Did he tell you much about the author?'

'No, only that she was a relative and insisted on anonymity. The book was to be credited as "By a Lady." I must stress that I did not want to publish this book, but I felt that to reject it would offend Mr Austen's friend, my valuable author. I certainly had no desire to invest in what I was sure would be a commercial failure, so I offered to publish it on commission.'

'Perhaps you would be kind enough to explain that to me.'

'Of course. The least risky business arrangement for both author and publisher is for the book to be published against guaranteed sales. This is achieved by the author or publisher persuading potential purchasers to subscribe to it in advance. As soon as there are sufficient subscribers to cover the costs of printing, the book is put into production. Depending on circumstances, the author receives either a royalty or a percentage of the profits. This arrangement was at one time very popular, but it involves a lot of what may appear to be begging letters to potential subscribers, and in recent years it has fallen out of favour.'

'Did you suggest it to Mr Austen?'

'Oh, yes. I had no intention of investing in his book. However, he was opposed to the suggestion, mainly on the grounds that success in obtaining subscriptions would surely depend on the author's identity being known.'

'Of course.'

'Another arrangement is for the publisher to buy the copyright in the work. He pays the author a mutually agreed sum of money in advance of publication or shortly after. This gives him the exclusive rights to publish the work for fourteen years for no additional payment. He takes all the risk and all the profit from the sales of the work. Some authors prefer this arrangement, especially if, as is often the case, they are in urgent need of money.'

'And the arrangement is popular with publishers?'

'That depends on the quality and commercial potential of the work and whether a mutually acceptable fee for the copyright can be negotiated.'

'Does that mean regardless of sales, the author never receives any further payment?'

'Occasionally, publishers will make further payments usually to ensure that they are offered further works by the author.'

'I understand. And the third arrangement?'

'That is publishing on commission. In short, the author pays the publisher to print, advertise and sell the work, and receives all the income from sales less a commission to the publisher of ten percent. This removes all risk from the publisher but reduces his potential income to very little.'

Sarah considered this and then said, 'So Mr Austen had to pay you to publish Miss Austen's novel.'

'That is correct.'

'Would it be possible for me to know the financial details?'

'I have them here in readiness.' Egerton opened a ledger and ran a finger down a column of figures.

'In this case, because Mr Austen was known to one of my authors and was a partner in a bank that had connections with various military organisations, I did not consider it necessary to ask him to pay any costs in advance. Now here we are. I accepted *Sense and Sensibility* in 1810 and it was available for purchase the following year. Typesetting and printing costs for 750 copies amounted to £150 with a further £24 spent on advertising. The book was priced at 15 shillings less a discount of a third to the trade. Sales income amounted to £356. I received a commission of £36. After deduction of all costs including our commission, the profit for the author was £140, and this was paid to Mr Austen early in 1812. At that time, we did not know that his sister was the author.'

'That is most interesting,' Sarah said. 'She did quite well out of it.'

'Indeed, yes. If I had taken all the risk, she would have been offered considerably less for the copyright. From my point of view, the income from the publication was hardly worth all the work involved. From the author's point of view, it had been a good deal. £140 for the first printing should have been very encouraging. It was unusually good, I was told, for a first novel by a totally unknown author. All copies were sold in less than two years.'

'Your advertising must have been very effective. Were there any reviews?'

'Two that I know of. Both favourable. One long one in *Critical* which included many extracts from the novel and a shorter in *The British Critic*. The good sales were really due, though, to the fact that we are also booksellers, and we supply many of the over 1,000 circulating libraries in the country.'

'Is that the main market for fiction?'

'Libraries and book clubs, yes. Books are expensive and beyond the pockets of most people. Inevitably a great deal of borrowing and sharing goes on. With the second book, *Pride and Prejudice,* I purchased the copyright in 1812 for £110. At the time, I did not expect sales to be large enough to be worth doing all the work on a commission basis.'

'And was Miss Austen—or her brother—happy with that, even though it was significantly less than she had earned from her first book for which she had retained the copyright?'

'Yes. I got the impression the author or her brother—it was difficult to know who was actually benefitting financially from the books—badly needed money. It also seemed to be important to publish the book without delay, even though she, or her brother, had nothing much to gain from its sales. She stood to earn nothing more and the book would be "By a Lady, the author of *Sense and Sensibility.*" I had very little expectations from it and, much to Miss Austen's annoyance, was rather slow in bringing it out.' Egerton smiled wryly. 'I received several somewhat tart letters from her demanding an explanation for the delay and insisting that I publish the book immediately.'

'Which you then did.'

Egerton nodded. Consulting the ledger again, he said, 'It did rather better than the first novel, selling 1,000 copies of the first printing and 750 of a second. It received three good reviews. I believe, though, I heard that a number of people took exception to the character of Elizabeth Bennet. She was not the kind of meek heroine they were used to.' He laughed. 'Apparently, some readers considered her behaviour towards Mr Darcy quite shameful.'

'Did you ever meet Miss Austen?' Sarah asked.

'Yes. She called on me to discuss the publication of her third novel, *Mansfield Park*.'

'What did you think of her?'

'I thought her a strange woman. Very cold and diffident. She seemed to lack all interest in her work except what it could earn for her. She had no interest in discussing her writing. Unlike many other authors, she did not want to talk about her plans for the future. She was very sarcastic, even cruel, about the novels of other women writers. She was especially critical of Mrs Radcliffe's very popular gothic stories. To be blunt, I found her unattractive in every way. She dressed drably and unfashionably, had no social conversation, and had rather a mean little face, I thought. And she could have been selling me soap for all she had to say about her writing. I really did not want to have further dealings with her, but *Pride and Prejudice* had been profitable, and I decided that if she would accept the same amount for the copyright of the new novel, *Mansfield Park*, I was prepared to publish it. She declined the offer and insisted that I publish it on commission. I was far from happy with this, especially as she still insisted on not being identified as the author. I decided that it would be the last book I took from her on this basis. She had shown herself to be a very troublesome author, always complaining, usually by letter, about delays and sending her brother to persuade the printer to hurry up getting proofs to her.'

'So you published it on commission.'

'Yes. It sold 1,250 copies and earned £310 for her. She was beginning to do quite well from her writing.'

'So after *Mansfield Park* you had no further dealings with her.'

'That is correct. She moved to John Murray.' Egerton smiled. 'That dour Scot would have not given way to her; of that I was sure. He would want the copyrights.'

'Why do you think she went to him?'

'He is Lord Byron's publisher, and his business is much larger than mine. He brings out over 200 titles a year.'

'Are those titles mostly fiction?'

'No. His fiction list is small. But there's quality there. It was probably a sensible move for her.'

When the time came for Sarah to leave, she said, 'Mr Egerton, you have been extraordinarily helpful. I am deeply obliged to you. You have provided me with some valuable insights into the book trade and Miss Austen's first experiences with it. May I ask just one more question?'

'Please do. I will be happy to help with anything.'

'Would you tell me about Mr Austen? He seems to have been her agent.'

'Oh, he was more than that. He supervised the printing of the two books I published on commission and, I think, was initially prepared to finance them. But his situation changed. He was very ill for most of 1812, and then, with hostilities dying down with the French, he had less business with the military. In 1815 his bank failed. He left London, a broken, bankrupt man and took holy orders. I believe he obtained a curacy at Chawton, the village in Hampshire where Miss Austen lived with her mother and, I think, a sister. I liked Henry Austen. He was a decent, amiable and straight-forward man. I much preferred dealing with him than with his sister.'

'Does he have a wife and children?'

'His wife, who was a French countess, I believe, died about five years ago. There were no children of whom he spoke.'

'It seems that a visit to Chawton will be necessary.' Sarah stood. 'I would like to purchase a complete set of the novels, including those published by John Murray if you have them in stock. Please send them to my address in Portman Place.' She handed Egerton her card and took out her purse to pay for the books.

Egerton waved the money away. Completely captivated by Sarah's charm and intelligence, as well as by her theatrical fame, he was determined to maintain a good impression of himself and of his business. He thought it possible that he might later persuade her to allow him to publish her plays. Play scripts by successful writers were in demand by the many families, often of the aristocracy, who indulged in play readings and amateur dramatics.

Chapter Five

While taking a chair back to Portman Place, Sarah resolved to put all thoughts of Jane Austen out of her mind. She had a play to rewrite before becoming further involved in the investigation of the author's life and works. After several hours of writing, she might have time to relax with one of Jane Austen's novels. She had already read *Sense and Sensibility* and *Pride and Prejudice* and enjoyed them both, especially the latter novel. Its lively and often witty dialogue would make a great play. She decided that on the coming Sunday, she would go with her friend Elizabeth to Winchester, and from there to Chawton where Henry Austen might agree to talk to her.

She had forgotten to ask Elizabeth whether she had read any of the novels, so she decided to ask one of her father's office messengers to take her copies of the first two. Elizabeth could read them while she rewrote her play. They would then be able to discuss the books during the long journey by coach from London to Winchester.

Sarah found the effort of asking intelligent questions about a subject she knew little or nothing about exhausting, especially after the rather troubling visit to the theatre and then the anxiety over whether the Reverend Clarke could help her with the Lord Chamberlain's office. Overcome by tiredness, she sat back in the chair and closed her eyes. By the time she reached home she was ready for a light dinner and an early night. She needed to be fully refreshed for the morning's writing. Her plays were popular because they were amusing and rich in witty dialogue. Unfortunately, being witty to order was much more difficult than being tragic or dramatic. Often, she stared for what seemed like hours at the wall of the library, almost praying for something clever to pop into her head that would get a laugh from an audience. Her best lines popped in as if from nowhere. They arrived fully clothed, as it were, all ready to be spoken. She couldn't help wondering if Egerton's description of Jane Austen as a tight-faced, simply dressed spinster was accurate. If it was, she thought, the woman could not possibly have written

Pride and Prejudice. It was all rather odd, especially when one took into consideration the author's determination to remain anonymous.

Sarah also realised that *Sense and Sensibility* may not have been the author's first book. She could have a pile of manuscripts that were either unfinished, completed but rejected by publishers, or never even submitted. Other Jane Austen novels might have been published under a pseudonym. At this stage, she felt unable to come to any conclusion about the author, and it was likely that the more Sarah discovered, the more she would realise how much more there was to learn. Only time and questioning a lot of people would, if she were lucky, provide at least some answers. What she needed to find and read, she concluded, was Jane Austen's journal. It would contain much that she needed to know. She wondered in whose possession it was and whether she would be allowed access to it.

When the chair arrived at her Portman Place home, she paid the chairmen and went inside.

As she passed the door of James's room, he looked up from what he was reading and said, 'Feel like a brandy? I have things to tell you.'

'A splendid idea. I'll organise them and see you in the drawing room. Give me ten minutes.'

When they had settled with their drinks in the comfortable high-backed chairs, James said, 'I hope you don't mind, Sarah, and I'm not for a minute wanting to interfere, but I thought I'd save you from what could be a long and profitless task.'

'Go on,' Sarah said, knowing that James was incapable of not becoming involved somehow in the Jane Austen project.

'Well, it occurred to me that Jane Austen, like most authors, would probably have approached a number of publishers before finding one who would take her on. I thought it might be useful—though I admit I don't know how—to know whom she approached and with what.'

'You've been reading my mind again, James,' she said with a laugh. 'Thank goodness we're not married. I couldn't bear to be such an open book to the man with whom I lived. Without some mystery, I'm just one more out of work actress.'

'Precisely,' James said. 'So I sent one of the apprentices around the town to check with booksellers and publishers as to whether they had had any dealings with either Jane or her brother, Henry. More about him in a minute. I told the lad to begin with the Minerva Circulating Library. It's not only the largest in the country but it's also owned by the Minerva Press which publishes more fiction written by and for women than most of the others put together.'

'I know it,' Sarah said. 'It's in Leadenhall Street.'

'Correct. Anyway, they hadn't been approached by anyone by the name of Austen, but they gave the lad the names of several publishers and booksellers who might have been offered something. The lad set off on what he was sure was going to be a wild goose chase. After all, there are scores of places to visit. But the assistant at Minerva had been sufficiently helpful to list the possibilities in the order of the most likely. The lad was lucky. Out of the first dozen he called on, two remembered being approached by an Austen. A man working for Cadell and Davies, a highly successful publisher of fiction, remembered receiving a parcel from Jane's father, the Reverend George Austen of Steventon Rectory, in about 1797 or perhaps a year or so later. Having been instructed not to accept, and therefore have to pay the carriage on what was clearly an unsolicited manuscript, and, thinking from the return address that it was probably a book of sermons, he returned it to sender unopened. He didn't even read any covering letter that might have been inside the parcel.'

'He'll be kicking himself now,' Sarah said.

'Very likely. But it might have been sermons, of course.'

'1797.' Sarah did a quick mental calculation. 'Jane would have been twenty-two. The manuscript could have been her first novel. I wonder if it was.'

'We may never know. Crosby and Company are another publisher who were offered a novel "By a Lady". Crosby admits to having purchased the copyright of a novel called *Susan* for ten pound in 1802.'

'When did he publish it?'

'He didn't. He never got around to doing it. It was listed in his catalogue for that year as "In the press," but it never appeared. He doesn't think much of it, apparently. It's a sort of gothic novel, but not in the least exciting. He told our lad that his reader said that it takes half the book before the plot gets going. He decided not to risk money on it.'

'So it will just rot forever in his office.'

'Seems like it.'

'That's a shame, isn't it?'

'Yes, but he said he'd be willing to release the copyright for what he paid for it. And he's told the author that.'

'Jane?'

'No. Henry Austen, acting as agent, made the contact.'

'This is really interesting, James. You are clever to have sent the lad around.'

'I gave him a shilling for a pie and ale and extra shoe leather,' James said with a laugh. 'He's had a great day. He's fast asleep in his room now.'

'Anything else?'

'No. He can call on some more tomorrow, but I doubt if there'll be anything more of interest.'

'Henry Austen,' Sarah said, remembering that James had said he would talk about him later.

'Yes. Henry Austen. And his brother, James. They published a weekly magazine called *The Loiterer*. It ran for over fifty issues. I understand that they wrote most of it themselves.'

'Did it serialise fiction?'

'I don't know. I doubt it. I think it was probably inspired by Johnson's *The Idler*. It all happened a long time ago. They were both students at Oxford at the time. It was a very considerable achievement. I assume that after a year they ran out of money. James left Oxford and became a clergyman. Henry stayed in the city and joined the Oxford Militia.'

'When was this?'

'1789.'

'One thing is becoming clear,' Sarah said. 'The family is obviously literary. I suppose it could be possible that either James or Henry authored the novels. Men hiding their identity behind a dress.'

'Yes. Especially given the nature of the novels.'

'But assuming that their sister, Jane, is the author, why did she insist on anonymity?'

'That is something to be discovered. And was the parcel from George Austen just a collection of his sermons or was it his daughter's novel or one of his son's, and if it were one of Jane's, then which one?'

'This project is beginning to look like a jigsaw puzzle, James, but one for which we keep finding new pieces. A puzzle that can never be finished.' Sarah

finished her drink and stood. 'James, I'm so grateful
to you for your help. Don't hesitate to follow your
journalist's and lawyer's instincts. I'm going to need
all the help and advice I can get.' She bent down and
kissed James on the cheek. Then went to bed.

~

James poured himself another brandy, sipped some
slowly, and wondered, for perhaps the thousandth
time, what it would be like to have Sarah for a wife.
He told himself at least the same number of times
that the situation between them was perfect as it was.

Chapter Six

Sarah rose early and set about the task of revising the play. At first, despairing of being able to make an extra scene or two work, she destroyed the whole of her first draft, then, suddenly, she realised how she could complicate the plot in such a way that it required more scenes. After that, the lines flowed from her pen nib. They were not, she thought, especially good lines, but they would be acceptable when spoken by the great Edmund Kean, assuming he was not drunk at the time.

While one of the clerks in the office undertook the task of copying the extra scenes and the amended existing ones, she set off for Cheyne Walk to make arrangements with Elizabeth for their departure for Winchester. They met in a nearby coffee shop.

'I suggest we take a mail coach to Winchester,' Sarah said when they'd relaxed with their coffee. 'They are the fastest, and if we travel at night, the road will be less busy. There's a coach that leaves the Bell and Crown in Holborn every evening at eight o'clock. It's about sixty miles to Winchester, so allowing for changing the horses several times, but without any upsets or other problems, we should reach Winchester in time for breakfast the following morning. We'll sit inside. We still won't get much sleep, but at least we'll be dry if it rains.'

Elizabeth said, 'Where shall we stay?'

'I suggest we stay in the city. It's an old Roman town and full of history. We may need to be in the district for some time. I've heard there is a fine inn, The King's Head. We'll take the best room and use it as our base. Is that all right, dear?'

'Yes, of course. Will we share? I won't feel happy on my own in a hotel.'

Sarah laughed, reached across the table for her friend's hand, and said, 'You're a bit of a nervous goose, aren't you? Of course we'll share. It's what all friends do when they travel together. It's part of the fun.'

Gratefully, Elizabeth squeezed the proffered hand. Sarah smiled and thought, not for the first time, how young her friend was, if not in years, then in maturity. Before her father, the master of a privateer, had died at sea, she had received an education at home from a governess. Then, while still a girl and her father having left only a small provision in his will, she had had to provide for her mother. She'd spent a year with a family in Florence—old friends of her father's—and there learned to be an engraver. On her return to England, she had obtained employment on a magazine. It had involved long, lonely hours of work, leaving no time or money for a social life. Realising that there was only a future of years and years as a lowly engraver until her eyesight gave out, she had decided at the age of twenty to try to earn a better living as a portrait painter. The increasing number of merchants and tradesmen with social pretensions and the money to assist them, was creating a demand for cheap portraits. Until turning to portrait painting, she had lived almost as a recluse with only her mother as a companion, but knowing that such work would not come to her, she had taken her small savings and, with frugal living, rented the top-floor apartment in Cheyne Walk. Although she'd acquired clients and was beginning to enjoy a small reputation as a portrait artist, she felt lonely in London and starved of affection. She had needed a close woman friend who would understand her and have time to spend enjoying life with her.

In contrast, Sarah, who was also an only child, was sophisticated and self-confident, with a large number of acquaintances but no close woman friend. The women had met each other at the best possible time for them both. For so many men and women trying to make a living in the arts, whether from painting, music, the theatre or literature, there was little time for close friends. Such people craved even one close friend who could be relied on to be readily available and have the sensibility to be able to lend an understanding ear. And to share any real empathy and understanding, they needed to be of one's own sex.

After sipping her coffee, Sarah said, 'Until Jane Austen went to stay in Winchester in the last few days or weeks of her life, she lived with her mother and older sister at Chawton, which is just a morning's journey from Winchester. Until he retired, her father was the rector at Steventon, which is where Jane was born and grew up. Both Chawton and Steventon are about the same distance from Basingstoke, so we could visit one, stay overnight, and visit the other on our way home.'

'You're so well organised, and well-informed, dearest.'

Sarah replied, 'I'm fortunate to live with a father and a friend who spend their lives digging out information. And the journal employs several young reporters to help them. I'll come with a hackney to collect you at six-thirty on Sunday evening. Don't bring much luggage. The mail coaches don't have room for more than one bag per passenger. If we have to stay away longer, we can always send for more clothes or buy anything we need. Now I must run. I have to get my play to Carlton House before the Reverend Clarke goes home for the day.'

The women kissed goodbye, and Sarah took a hackney to collect the amended scripts from the office at Portland Place, and then on to Carlton House. On her arrival, Clarke received her warmly and promised to use his best offices to get the play approved as soon as possible. In return, Sarah agreed to keep him informed of anything of particular significance that she discovered about Jane Austen. Then she went home via the Bell and Crown at Holborn where she bought inside tickets for the Sunday evening mail to Winchester. The investigation was about to begin in earnest.

Chapter Seven

Neither Sarah nor Elizabeth slept much on the overnight mail coach to Winchester, and as soon as they arrived at The King's Head, they went straight to bed, waking up just in time for a late lunch. Afterwards they walked to the cathedral to look around and plan their strategy for the next day. As things turned out, very little planning was necessary. They hadn't been inside the magnificent building for more than a few moments before an elderly man, bent almost double and dressed in a cassock that was so worn that it seemed to be turning green in the faint rays of the watery afternoon sun, shuffled towards them from the shadows as if he'd been hiding in wait, which he probably had. Sarah suspected that he haunted the cathedral and preyed on visitors not so much for gratuities, though these would always be welcomed, as for conversation. Her gentle questioning elicited the information that he had devoted his life to the service of the cathedral, initially as a chorister, boy and man, then as a sacristan. Sarah presumed that he had neither the education nor appropriate fortune to attend a university, and had, therefore, never taken holy orders.

As he approached, he raised his head to look her in the face and said, 'Good afternoon, madam, are you looking to see anything in particular?'

'We were hoping to see where Jane Austen is buried,' Sarah told him. 'I'm writing an article about her, and my friend is an illustrator and engraver. She would like to make a sketch of the tombstone.'

'Follow me. The late Miss Austen is interred in a vault beneath the north aisle.'

'You are most kind.'

They followed the ancient, whose heavy breathing suggested that he was very near the end of his life.

They found Jane Austen's gravestone about halfway along the aisle. The cathedral didn't have enough light to read the inscription, so Elizabeth hurried to the entrance to buy a candle. While Sarah waited for her return, she questioned the old man, who stood panting as he recovered from the ordeal of a fifty-yard walk.

'Is this the Austen family grave?' she asked.

'Oh, no. Just of the single lady. Though the Austen family is a well-known Hampshire family.'

'Do you know why Miss Austen is buried in the cathedral?'

'Her brother was ordained here.'

'And that was enough to obtain a place in the cathedral for his sister's grave,' Sarah said unable to keep the surprise out of her voice. 'Surely many important local people would want a place.'

The old man shrugged. 'You will have to ask the Dean for the explanation. Perhaps he offered a large donation to the building fund.'

'Perhaps indeed. What does burial here cost?'

The old sacristan shrugged. 'Nearly a hundred pounds. But there won't be many more. There's no space left.' He cackled. 'The place is full of kings and queens and all kinds of saints going back to six-hundred and forty-two. People that's travelled do say that it's the largest cathedral in Europe.'

'Then the late Jane Austen is in good company.'

Sarah looked about her at the vast building. 'It is certainly very large.' Then taking the topic firmly back to Jane Austen, she asked, 'Was it a well-attended funeral? I suppose it must have been to have cost so much.' One hundred pounds was almost, she realised, as much as the price the publishers paid Jane for the copyright of *Pride and Prejudice*.

'Four gentlemen.'

'I beg your pardon.'

'I said four gentlemen. They followed the coffin down College Street from where the lady died in lodgings.'

Sarah thought this extraordinary—not that there were no women mourners; women rarely attended funerals as it was a common belief that the ceremony was too emotionally upsetting for them to bear. It was the paucity of mourners that surprised her. She wondered who the four gentlemen had been. They would go straight to the top of her list of relatives and friends to be interviewed.

'Presumably,' she said, 'the Dean will have the gentlemen's names and addresses.'

'Or the Precentor. He read the service.' The old man cackled again. 'He had to be quick. The congregation were already coming in for the morning service.'

This brought the conversation to an end as Elizabeth returned with a lighted candle and they read the words carved on Jane Austen's gravestone. Sarah could hardly believe what she read. She read it over again, her years as an actress making it a simple matter for her to commit them to memory. Elizabeth copied them into her sketch book and made a brief drawing of the gravestone's position in the cathedral.

The inscription read:

In Memory of
JANE AUSTEN,
youngest daughter of the late
Reverend GEORGE AUSTEN
formerly Rector of Steventon in this County.
She departed this life on the 18th July 1817
aged 41, after a long illness, supported with
the patience and hopes of a Christian.

The benevolence of her heart,
the sweetness of her temper, and
the extraordinary endowments of her mind
obtained the regard of all who knew her and
the warmest love of her intimate connections.

Their grief is in proportion to their affection.
They know their loss to be irreparable, but
in their deepest affliction they are consoled
by a firm though humble hope that her charity,
devotion, faith and purity have rendered
her soul acceptable in the sight of her
REDEEMER

'Remarkable,' Sarah said, giving Elizabeth a look
as if to tell her to reserve any comments until later.

To the retired sacristan she said, 'Do you know much about the family?'

'I believe they are an old Hampshire family with connections to the church. It's who you know that's important, isn't it?'

'It certainly can be.'

Deciding that the old man had told her everything he knew, Sarah resisted the temptation to ask further questions. Anything else he said would be no more than speculation and third or fourth-hand gossip. The only gossip worth having would be from people who really knew the family—villagers, parishioners and a few friends and acquaintances wanting to show off their intimacy with the family.

'You have been most kind,' she said, discreetly pressing a coin into his trembling hand. 'I may want to talk to you again. For now, we bid you good afternoon.'

She stood and nodded to Elizabeth, who closed her sketch book and returned it with her pencil to her artist's bag.

The women left the cathedral quietly, leaving an appropriate offering as they did so. One never knew who was watching one in such places. Sarah thought it was possible they would need to return, perhaps to try to find out from the Dean why an insignificant spinster had been granted a final resting place of such an honour.

As they left the cathedral precincts and walked towards the town, Sarah told Elizabeth what the old man had said. She finished by saying, 'It was not only interesting, but wholly unexpected. I'm not going to draw any conclusions from what we've learned. The last thing we should do is to develop any theories too soon and then attempt to make the facts we discover fit our theories. At this stage we are simply gathering information and storing it away.'

'It is all so strange. Such a small funeral,' Elizabeth said. 'There would surely have been more than a few people locally who have read her books and would have attended her funeral.'

'If there had been a funeral notice. I suspect there wasn't. What I would like you to do tomorrow, dear, is visit all the local newspapers offices and jot down all such notices and any obituaries. Winchester is an important city, and all the Hampshire papers will have offices here, if only to accept advertisements and news items. It won't surprise me to discover there were no funeral notices. If there had been, I think, as you say, attendance would have been larger. Perhaps even a reporter would have covered it.'

Sarah hoped this was the case. A local reporter would have taken great care to obtain as many names as possible. Newspapers were highly competitive and listing the names of people who attended functions was a great aid to circulation figures.

Delighted to have a specific task, Elizabeth said, 'I'm happy to do that, dearest. And you?'

'If the Dean can spare a few minutes, I will ask him for the names and addresses of the mourners and if he can provide the name of the doctor who attended Jane at the end. Now I suggest we go back to the hotel and rest for a while before we have some supper.'

The rest turned out to be not just for a while. They both fell asleep instantly and did not awake until the noise of coaches loading and departing from the hotel woke them early the next morning.

Chapter Eight

After an early breakfast, Sarah and Elizabeth
separated to do their respective tasks. Elizabeth
discovered three local newspapers, each with an
office in the centre of the town. Two of the papers
were also printed locally, *The Hampshire Chronicle and
Courier* and *The Courier*.

The item in *The Hampshire Chronicle and Courier*
was very brief. It read:

Winchester, Saturday July 19th: Died yesterday,
in College Street, Miss Jane Austen, youngest
daughter of the late Rev. George Austen, formerly of
Steventon, in this county.

The notice in *The Courier*, published several days
later on the twenty-second of July, was more

informative and had been written and handed in by Cassandra Austen. It stated:

On the 18th inst. at Winchester, Miss Jane Austen, youngest daughter of the late Rev. George Austen, Rector of Steventon, in Hampshire, and the authoress of Emma, Mansfield Park, Pride and Prejudice and Sense and Sensibility. Her manners were most gentle; her affections ardent; her candour was not to be surpassed, and she lived and died as became a humble Christian.

The notice in *The Hampshire Telegraph and Sussex Chronicle* was, Elizabeth thought, so brief and blunt as to be discourteous. It stated simply:

'On Friday last died, Miss Austen, late of Chawton, in this County.'

None of the papers published funeral notices, and from this Elizabeth deduced that whichever brother had organised the funeral had made certain that only the immediate family should know about it. She could not help thinking, in spite of Sarah's warning not to speculate, that this was odd. Jane Austen, as the daughter of the former Rector of Steventon would surely have had childhood friends, if only among immediate neighbours. The daughter of a local clergyman would almost certainly have been invited to the various balls and other social functions held in the great houses in the district.

While Elizabeth visited the offices of the newspapers, Sarah went first to the Cathedral Close to call on the Precentor of the cathedral, the Reverend Thomas Watkins. He was also the Chaplain of Winchester College and over the years had had dealings with the Austen family and had conducted the funeral. He received Sarah cordially and helpfully provided the information she required.

'The four gentlemen who followed the coffin from her lodgings in College Street were three of her brothers, Edward, Henry and Francis with her nephew, Edward's son, James. Edward Austen Knight has a large property at Chawton where his mother and his sister Cassandra reside in a cottage on the property. He and his large family do not live there, however. Their family seat is at Godmersham in Kent. Henry Austen has a curacy at St Nicholas Church in Chawton, though he lodges outside of the village. I have an address for him.'

He turned towards a desk and reached across for a pen, with which he dipped in the ink and copied the address onto a small slip of paper. After powdering the ink dry, he handed the note to Sarah and said, 'Another brother, Revd James Austen, is now the Rector of Steventon. He lives with his wife at the rectory. He did not attend the funeral as he is seriously ill.'

'I suppose the family are well known in the district,' Sarah said.

'Very much so,' the Precentor replied. 'The Reverend George Austen and his wife had several children of their own, and for many years, the rectory hosted a small boarding school for boys, several of whom later attended Winchester College.'

'Was it widely known locally, do you think, that Jane Austen had become a highly regarded novelist?' Sarah asked.

'By local people who read novels, perhaps. But I understand that until very recently, the late Miss Austen published much of her work anonymously. The first I knew about her being an authoress was when I read the small obituary in *The Courier*. It came as quite a shock to me. Mind you,' the Precentor added, 'I suppose I should not have been surprised. The Reverend George Austen was a well-educated man and not just in ecclesiastical matters. He had a fine library which I believe included many works of fiction. No doubt his children were encouraged to make good use of it. Henry and James are both of a literary inclination.'

'This is most interesting,' Sarah said. 'I look forward to meeting Mr Henry Austen and also Miss Cassandra Austen at Chawton. I also intended visiting Steventon with my friend, Miss Stockton. She is an illustrator interested in drawing and painting country scenes. I would like to see where Jane Austen spent her early years.'

'That would be interesting for you. However, as I am sure you appreciate, Miss Cassandra and her mother are still in deep mourning. I doubt if they will receive visitors, other than the closest of family friends.'

'Of course,' Sarah said. 'I would not dream of intruding.'

The clergyman smiled. 'I did not want you to make the journey and be disappointed. Fortunately, both villages are not too far from Basingstoke. They are pleasant enough, but Steventon may not be easy to access by carriage at this time of the year. As soon as you leave the turnpike, the road is little more than a muddy cart track and deeply rutted from the carriers' wagons. Your best plan would be to hire a chaise to Basingstoke, or even one of the regular coaches—there are several every day. If you ride,' he smiled knowingly, impressed by Sarah's aristocratic appearance, 'and I assume that you do, you can hire a horse to visit the villages. The weather is settled at present, and I am informed by my gardener, who is usually reliable about such things, that it is likely to be so for several days. A gentle ride along the country lanes should be very pleasant.'

'Your suggestions are most sensible. I am greatly obliged to you. Miss Stockton and I would need to stay overnight at Basingstoke. Can you recommend suitable accommodation?'

'The White Hart is a fine coaching inn and has a good reputation. I am confident you will find it acceptable accommodation for two ladies travelling alone.'

Sarah had one more question for the Precentor. 'If possible, I would like to speak to Jane's doctor. Do you know where I can find him?'

'He is Doctor Lyford, and you will usually find him at our new city hospital. I understand Miss Austen came to stay in Winchester to be in his care.'

Sarah thanked the Reverend Watkins for his kindness in answering her questions and left his residence to walk to the hospital. She thought it unlikely that Dr Lyford would be free to see her, and, in any case, he would be very circumspect regarding what he told her about Jane's illness. However, having come so far, she reasoned that it would be a mistake to leave Winchester without following all possible avenues of inquiry.

As luck would have it, the doctor had just completed a surgical operation when she arrived at the hospital. He sat alone in his small office, writing up his notes on the procedure which had been sufficiently successful to put him in a relaxed state of mind. A tall, elegant man in his early fifties, he expressed no surprise when Sarah told him the purpose of her visit.

'I was Miss Austen's physician for some time,' he said, 'and when I moved here to take up the position in the new hospital, she continued to be my patient. I was aware of her novel writing. In fact, she insisted on writing until almost the end. She was truly dedicated to her work and was determined to leave behind as many books as she could.'

'Do you know what she was working on towards her last days?'

'Another novel. She told me it was inspired by a visit she had made some years before to Worthing.'

'That's a coastal town in Sussex, I believe.'

'Yes, for a time it was quite fashionable, but when the Prince Regent became interested in building his pavilion in Brighton, Worthing rather lost its popularity.'

'Thank you,' Sarah replied. 'That is interesting. Her executor may be able to arrange publication of her unfinished novel, depending how much progress she'd made before her illness finally prevented her from writing. Did she suffer much towards the end?'

Dr Lyford pondered the question for a moment before replying, 'She experienced pain only during her last few days. Prior to the onset of that pain, her symptoms were mainly fatigue and listlessness. A generalised feeling of being very unwell. To be honest, I do not know exactly what caused her death. I can say only that she showed all the signs of an infection, and that there was nothing medicine or surgery could do to prevent her vital organs from shutting down. Quite simply, she had an infection that got out of control and responded to nothing I, nor I believe, any doctor could do. One day perhaps we shall discover ways to combat this kind of infection, but at present, we are at a loss even to understand exactly what is happening.'

Sarah appreciated that Dr Lyford had told her as much as there was to know about Jane's final illness, so she offered him her hand. His remarks about the unfinished novel and Jane's attitude to her writing had been unexpected and possibly significant.

Well-pleased with the morning's meetings, Sarah walked back to the hotel, there to have a light lunch with Elizabeth and reserve inside seats on a coach to take them the twenty miles or so to Basingstoke, a journey of about three hours. According to the Precentor, from Basingstoke to Steventon or Chawton on horseback would be just over an hour's easy ride to either village. However, Sarah decided that on their arrival at Basingstoke, after resting for a while after the journey, it would be too late in the evening to visit either of the villages. A better plan, as the Precentor had suggested, would be to stay overnight at the White Hart Inn and continue to Steventon on the following day.

After explaining the situation to Elizabeth, she said, 'I don't want you to think we have to work all the time. If we find the place to our liking, we can stay and explore the district. And we don't even have to achieve anything. I would like our Jane Austen project to be as much a holiday as anything. We have never had one together.'

'That sounds wonderful,' Elizabeth said. 'I would like to paint some landscapes if we come across something that really appeals.'

And so it was settled. Little more than an hour later, they were seated in the afternoon coach to Basingstoke.

Chapter Nine

The coach was in excellent condition and made good time to Basingstoke where Sarah and Elizabeth found accommodation available at the White Hart Inn. After inspecting the room and finding it small but clean and comfortable with a large attractively canopied four-poster bed, Sarah asked for their bags to be sent up.

Before changing for dinner, they visited the stables next to the inn where they arranged to have two steady mounts for use throughout the next day. Sarah also arranged for the hotel to send a messenger to the nearby parish of Deane where Henry Austen had a lodging. Her sealed letter to him was short and to the point.

It had occurred to Sarah that a possible way of passing the evening would be to visit the local theatre. However, the landlord informed her that there was, as yet, no theatre in the town. The nearest located in Andover, ten miles away, and in his opinion, the quality of the theatre premises there and the standard of the performances were so poor as to be not worth a journey of even two miles, let alone ten. Sarah had no difficulty in accepting the landlord's advice. Accordingly, after their meal, the two women retired to their room and prepared for bed.

Sarah had brought with her both the novels, *Persuasion* and *Northanger Abbey*, and it was part of their plan to take it in turns to read a few chapters aloud each night before they went to sleep.

By the light of a bedside candle, Elizabeth read a few chapters from *Northanger Abbey*, then put down the book and said, 'It seems to me that the opening chapters contain little of interest: Before Isabella appears on the scene in the fourth chapter, it consists mainly of inconsequential dialogue between the insipid heroine, Catherine, and her family. After arriving in Bath, she befriends the equally shallow Isabella. Neither can be described as an interesting character. They are the epitome of the worst kind of heroine: timid, over-anxious to please, and totally lacking in confidence. Isabella seems obsessed with dress and frippery, together with all the silly social niceties while she is engaged in a desperate search for a suitable man to marry.'

'I think we need to consider,' Sarah suggested, 'that Miss Austen was satirising the kind of heroine that we frequently find in romances. I think we'll find that the whole book is a parody of the gothic novels that are so popular with members of the circulating libraries. The problem for Jane Austen, as I know from my experience as a playwright, is that it is difficult, even impossible, to satirise that which is boring without also being tedious.'

She knew only too well the way many plays that set out to satirise and parody situations or certain kinds of character often collapsed in the middle. The usual lack of plot and an excess of pointless dialogue amounted to little more than vocal noise to persuade the audience that the play was still being performed.

Elizabeth nodded. 'I know I may be missing something significant, dearest,' she said, 'but I have to confess that I don't think this is a good book. I'm not surprised that Lady Hertford finds it hard to accept that all the novels purportedly written by Jane Austen are in fact, all her own work. I really don't know how the author of this could be the same person who wrote *Pride and Prejudice*.'

'It certainly makes one think,' Sarah agreed. 'Though, perhaps, we should take account of the advertisement by the authoress.' Sarah took the book and tapped the text on the page. 'Here, the writer admits that *Northanger Abbey* is an earlier work.'

'Oh, I missed that,' Elizabeth confessed. 'I went straight to chapter one and read from there.'

'It does mean that we cannot assume her books have been published in the order they were written,' Sarah said. 'I have plays written years ago that I could not get performed. I put them away intending to revise them later. Some of them are so poor I shall not waste time on them. I think we need to try to obtain the dates when Jane Austen wrote each of her novels and the dates when she made fair copies of them with corrections and revisions.'

'I suppose,' Elizabeth said, 'many novelists have to make the final copies themselves because no one else can read their handwriting.'

'True. Or they cannot afford to pay a copyist.'

'It would be very interesting to compare an early version with the final printed version,' Elizabeth mused. 'Apart from an author's changes, there could be editorial changes to consider.'

Sarah laughed. 'Believe me, the final rehearsed version of my plays bears little relation to my first drafts, even to the version I have copied for the actors. I have to accept not only the changes demanded by the censor but also those inserted by actors who think they can write my lines better than I can. It's infuriating. I take immense trouble to write my lines carefully so that the stresses, places to pause, and rhythms and so on are where they should be, and then an actor who can't be bothered to learn what I've written just gets the gist of my meaning and paraphrases it. Do clients interfere with your paintings?'

'Frequently. If they don't like some aspect of what I've done, and they can afford it, they engage another artist to paint over it. One of my clients engaged me to paint his mistress of the time. When he tired of her or she of him, I never discovered which, he had her face over-painted with the face of her successor.'

'There we are then. Anything can be changed by other hands,' Sarah said. 'Literature, art or even music. Oh dear!' She yawned. 'It's time to sleep, I think. We may have a busy day tomorrow, beginning with a ride to Deane or Chawton.'

'If the weather is fine, that will be lovely. It's months since I was last on a horse, and I do so enjoy a good, long ride.'

Elizabeth closed the book, put it on the small bedside table, and extinguished the candle. 'What will you do if Henry Austen refuses to meet with you?' she asked, half whispering, as she settled comfortably.

'I was thinking about that during the journey this afternoon. I'm afraid we must expect to be made unwelcome by the family. They are obviously determined to avoid publicity. For whatever reason, they do not want Jane to be remembered for her novels. The absence of a funeral notice and an adequate obituary in the local press is further confirmation.'

'Perhaps Jane Austen's sister will be more helpful.'

'That's possible, but I think it may be inappropriate to approach her at this time. According to the Precentor, she and Mrs Austen are still in deep mourning. The brother, Henry, is in a different situation. He has been his sister's agent, has written and had published the extraordinary memoir about her, and he is presumably responsible for the wording on the gravestone. I think it is reasonable for me to approach him for information about his sister's life and works. He is obviously the spokesman for the family.' She yawned and slid further down the bed. 'Goodnight, my dear. Sleep well.'

The two friends kissed, turned on their sides and were soon asleep.

Chapter Ten

The next morning, as Sarah entered the dining room
for breakfast, the landlord approached her.

'The messenger returned with an answer to your
letter, madam,' he said, handing it to her.

Thanking him, Sarah took it but waited until she
was seated at a vacant table by the window before
opening it. The message was a single line.

Madam,

*I can meet you at 10 a.m. at Minerva's Rooms in
Basingstoke.*

Henry Austen.

Minerva was the largest chain of circulating libraries in the country. In the smaller towns the branches or franchises were usually more than just libraries. They had to be to be profitable so were often small department stores. Although books were becoming increasingly popular, sales and even loans were still largely dependent on the middle class. An annual subscription cost a minimum of two pounds, and even the penny or tuppence per week fee could be an extravagance for people who could not or did not want to subscribe, especially as fines were levied on late returns. A week was not usually long enough for many readers to finish a complete book.

When Elizabeth arrived at the breakfast table a few minutes later, Sarah passed her the note, explaining as she did so, 'That's rather more and less than I expected. More in that he's saving us a journey. Less in that he gives no indication that he is prepared to discuss his sister.'

'I expect he thinks Minerva's is neutral ground,' Elizabeth commented. 'We are lucky there is one here.'

After a leisurely breakfast, the two friends set off for Minerva's. They soon found the department store—for this is what it turned out to be—located in the High Street, and its façade gave the impression of being three smaller shops knocked together to form a much larger one. Inside, at the rear of the store, and by far the smallest part, was the lending library. It seemed to have only a few hundred books available, though doubtless, Sarah thought, a hundred or so more would be out on loan. The rest of the premises had counters serving groceries, a range of teas, perfumery, cutlery and crockery, various other domestic items, newspapers and periodicals, and most importantly from Elizabeth's point of view, stationery and basic artists' supplies. At least a quarter of the store, however, existed as a coffee house.

In spite of the early hour, the establishment was already busy. Clearly the social centre of the town, it was a convenient place for businessmen to conduct negotiations and for women to exchange gossip. Sarah thought that most of the smartly dressed sales assistants would have had at least an education in the classics and numeracy at a local grammar school for boys.

They entered the store, found a table vacant and hurried towards it. Once seated, they relaxed and amused themselves by commenting on the surrounding activity. When a servant approached, Sarah ordered coffee and said, 'We are expecting a reverend gentleman at ten o'clock. He may ask for me. My name is Miss Sarah Kedron. He is the Reverend Henry Austen.'

'I know the gentleman,' the servant said. 'He's a member of the library. I will bring him to you.'

Sarah thought this was interesting information. A Minerva library in a country town would contain mostly novels for women readers with little of interest to an Oxford graduate. She thought, therefore, that Henry Austen probably borrowed books for Jane Austen's sister and mother at Chawton.

Sarah believed that an understanding of the intricate network of relationships of the Steventon Austens to branches of the family, some close, others as distant as cousins several times removed, would be crucial to any understanding of Jane Austen's life. The large family had members scattered around the country in widely different social and financial circumstances. Sarah soon discovered how important family had been to Jane—she'd spent much of her time, and most of her extremely limited and precious money, travelling from one relation or family friend to another.

The store had so much to see and comment on that time soon passed and before they expected it, a church clock struck ten. As though he'd been awaiting this cue outside the door, Henry Austen entered. Immediately the servant walked up to him and indicated where Sarah was sitting. Henry approached, and when he reached their table, stopped and bowed. Sarah stood and extended her hand. She believed it was essential that he accept she was of his class and not a hack from Grub Street.

Henry Austen was a handsome but haggard-looking man in his late forties, but his grey-white hair made him look much older than his years. Had he been dressed differently, Sarah thought, he could have been a successful but ageing tragedian, and this impression was supported by his sonorous and considered speech. Sarah detected little warmth in the man.

They shook hands and after Henry accepted the invitation to join them, Sarah introduced Elizabeth as a London portrait artist and her travelling companion. Henry acknowledged her with a courteous though wan smile.

For a moment it seemed as if the meeting had promising potential. In this, however, Sarah's hopes were very quickly dashed.

'I am greatly obliged, of course, for your interest in my dear late sister,' Henry Austen said as though reading from a prepared script, 'but I must make it absolutely clear to you, that we, by which I mean her family, have no wish for her to be remembered as the novelist. This is not what she wanted. Her life was devoted to the care of her mother, who has been an invalid for many years, and to the interests of her nieces of whom she was very fond. She wrote as a form of relaxation from her domestic and religious obligations as a devout Christian and a member of the Anglican persuasion. She sought neither fame nor fortune as a novelist. Indeed, she actively tried to avoid achieving it.'

'You have made that clear on the memorial stone and elsewhere,' Sarah said. 'But the question that has to be asked, sir, is: if that is so, why did she seek publication, even to the extent of investing capital in some of her books? They were published, I have been told, on a commission basis. This means that she had to accept responsibility for any losses the books incurred.'

'I must accept responsibility for her publications,' Henry said, a profound sadness in his voice, a deep melancholy. 'I seriously misunderstood my sister's wishes with regard to her writing. As I have misunderstood so many things. There is really no more to be said. I beseech you to ignore my sister's works. They were worthless to her. Choose another author to help you fill the pages of your periodical. Allow my dear sister to rest in peace and her family to grieve their terrible loss.'

Sarah opened her mouth to speak, but Henry denied her the opportunity.

'Do not, I beg you, approach my sister Cassandra. She is overwhelmed with grief. And bear in mind that only she really understood Jane. She is her executor and possesses all her papers but will insist their contents remain private to our immediate family. You will be wasting your time and causing a great deal of pain if you persist in your inquiries. I bid you good day. May God go with you.' With this, he stood up, bowed, turned and hurried from the room.

For several moments, Sarah felt too puzzled and moved to speak. Elizabeth had sufficient sensibility to remain silent. When Sarah did speak, it was very quietly and for Elizabeth's ears alone. 'I think he is ill. Not just physically. He seems to be overwhelmed by sadness and, I think, but I am not sure why, a sense of guilt.'

Elizabeth whispered in reply, 'Do you think he is telling the truth about Jane's intentions and wishes?'

Sarah paused and thoughtfully bit her lip. 'I truly don't know. It's possible, though from the little her first publisher had to say, I think it's very unlikely. We won't know for certain until we discover more about Henry Austen, and if we discover anything, I am not at all sure that we will like it.'

Still concerned about Henry Austen's abruptness, Elizabeth said, 'He gives the impression of being a defeated, emotionally dead man.'

Sarah put a hand on Elizabeth's arm. 'My dear, we could return to London this morning, if you wish. But as we have horses available, and we have not had the ride to Chawton, we could ride to Steventon instead. Even if we cannot speak to a member of the family, you could sketch the house where Jane lived for half her life. I might find someone in the village who knew her.'

'I think that's a lovely idea. I'll make a series of quick sketches of the church as well. I can work them up later.'

Sarah smiled with relief. 'I'm so pleased. Spring is here, and every day is getting warmer. A ride in the country will do us both good. We'll take the first coach to London tomorrow. There is nothing further for us here. Although we may have to come back if Cassandra Austen is willing to talk to us. I believe that most of Henry Austen's adult life has been spent in London and Oxford. That's where we are most likely to find out why he is in the state he is.' She paused, smiled wryly and then added, 'Assuming, that is, that we ever can find out. I am beginning to think that the Austen family has something to hide.'

'Show me a family that hasn't,' Elizabeth said. 'And I must say that I found our meeting with Henry Austen as disturbing. There is something very wrong in that man's life.'

'Yes. Very wrong.' Sarah stood. 'Perhaps we'll find out something about him at Steventon. He would have lived there until he left for university. There will be people in the village who know him even if family members won't talk to us. Come, let's go back to the hotel and change into suitable clothes for riding.'

The two women left Minerva's and returned to the hotel where Sarah ordered the hired horses to be made ready.

Chapter Eleven

The ride to Steventon was as pleasant and uneventful as Sarah had expected it would be. Their horses, only too used to the ill-treatment they suffered from casual hirers, responded well to the two women's firm but gentle management, and seemed to go out of their way to provide a comfortable journey, despite the unevenness and generally poor condition of the country lanes.

They arrived at the rectory just after noon. After dismounting in the lane outside the rectory, they let the horses graze on the fresh grass while they stood for several minutes admiring the house and its surroundings and wondering what their next move should be. Unlike many rural parishes, Steventon was substantial and included a number of wealthy families whose regular attendance at the church provided adequate funds for the upkeep of the church and of the house. Added to this was the regular income from the glebe farm.

Before Elizabeth had time to set up her easel and prepare her pencils, a young man of nineteen or so rode up suddenly and reined in his panting horse. He raised his hat to the women.

'Good day to you, ladies. May I be of any assistance? I am James Austen.' He smiled. 'Not yet the reverend. He is my father.'

'We are delighted to meet you,' Sarah said. 'I am Sarah Kedron and my companion is the artist Elizabeth Stockton.'

'Who is about to draw my family home,' James said. 'Please feel free to enter the garden if you wish.'

'Thank you. We are obliged to you,' Elizabeth said with a slightly coquettish smile. She realised, as did Sarah, that with the right approach, the young man might be a way to his parents.

'I should explain,' Sarah said, 'that I am writing a series of articles on women novelists of the Regency for *The Inquirer*. My first article will be about your lateaunt, Jane, who, in my opinion, is by far the most interesting of them all. Her death is a tragic loss in so many ways.'

James Austen dismounted and said, 'I would like to invite you into the house to meet my parents, but my father is gravely ill. I do not think my mother is prepared to receive visitors.'

'We completely understand. Please convey our condolences to her and to your father on their sad loss.'

Elizabeth cleverly added, 'We had the honour and pleasure of meeting your uncle Henry earlier today. He very graciously rode to see us in Basingstoke.'

'Ah,' James said, non-committally. 'Yes.'

Smiling, Sarah said, 'Would it be an imposition if I asked you just a few questions about your aunt?'

'I did not know her well,' James told her. 'She left here with my grandparents and her sister, my aunt Cassandra, very soon after her father retired. That was in about 1801. He was the rector here then. I was only three years old. They went to live in Bath for a few years—my grandfather died there soon after—and then they lived briefly in Southampton before settling at Chawton. My father inherited the living here, and Aunt Jane visited from time to time, but her visits were usually hurried and, of course, I was very young.' He grinned. 'She was a great traveller but rarely stayed long in the same place. There are branches of the family all over southern England.' He laughed. 'So many that one need not go to the expense of having a home of one's own. One could live on the hospitality of relatives.'

'Did she ever talk about her work?' Sarah asked, as much to keep the conversation going as anything.

'Not to me, but I know she did to several of her nieces, Fanny and Anne especially. They told me that they were interested in writing themselves. She encouraged them and offered advice. I believe she was very generous with her time and enjoyed the company of young people.' Smiling apologetically, he concluded, 'My own interests are of a more rural nature—hunting and shooting. I have no literary ambitions.'

'But you will, no doubt, go to Oxford,' Sarah said.

James nodded. 'Very likely. I am intended for the church.'

At this moment, the door of the rectory opened and a middle-aged woman, dressed in black, appeared. She took in the scene at the garden gate and then, as though coming to a sudden decision, hurried towards them. Sarah and Elizabeth exchanged glances. The expression on the woman's face was not welcoming.

'Ah! Here comes my mother,' James Austen said. 'Please excuse me.'

Dropping the reins of his horse, he entered the garden and approached his mother. They held a brief, half-whispered conversation, during which Mrs Austen's face gradually relaxed. She accompanied her son to the gate where after bidding Sarah and

Elizabeth, 'Good day,' he led his horse further down the lane and into the stables yard.

Mrs Austen approached them.

'Good day, ladies. I am Mrs James Austen,' she said. 'I do apologise for not being able to invite you into the house and offer you refreshments, but Mr Austen is extremely ill. My son was just returning from Basingstoke where he'd collected laudanum from the apothecary to ease his father's pain.'

Sarah expressed regret for their intrusion, but Mary Austen waved away the apology and said, 'Usually, I would have made you very welcome and been happy to talk to you about Jane. If only to put the record straight.'

This, Sarah thought, was a very telling remark that could be full of significance, but before she could speak, Mary Austen continued, 'I grew up with Jane. My family, the Lloyds, were neighbours, and we spent almost as much time in the Austen home as we did in our own. Jane and I were the closest of friends for many years. My sister, Martha, lives with Mrs Austen and Cassandra at Chawton. Anything you wish to know about Jane's childhood and early writing, I can tell you. But not at present. May I suggest you contact me in a week's time? By then I pray that my husband will have recovered.'

'You are most kind. I will do as you suggest.'

Sarah handed Mary Austen one of her cards.

'Kedron,' Mrs Austen said. 'Any relation to the publisher of *The Inquirer*?'

'My father.'

'Oh, my husband will be so pleased to meet you. Your father is one of his heroes. When he was at Oxford with his brother Henry, they published—and I believe they also wrote every word of it—a magazine. They were inspired by Samuel Johnson's *The Idler* and called their magazine *The Loiterer*. It was considered a remarkable achievement for two students. It ran for over fifty issues.'

At this point in the conversation a servant came out from the rear of the house, carrying a tray bearing glasses of lemonade. Grateful for the refreshment, Sarah and Elizabeth chatted to Mary Austen about the weather, the journey from Basingstoke and other neutral topics. They anticipated that, with care in what they said and asked her, Mary Austen could be an invaluable source of information.

Less than ten minutes later, they were on their way back to Basingstoke, satisfied with their visit to Steventon. Sarah felt confident that a door which she had feared would be closed to her, seemed to be wide open. Only a little patience and tact would be required.

Chapter Twelve

During the coach journey as they returned to London, Sarah said, 'I need to spend a few days in London before we set off again. I'll give you at least a couple of days' notice when I'm ready to leave. You do want to accompany me, don't you?'

'Of course, I do. Don't worry. I'll be ready to leave. It's been so interesting and enjoyable so far. Do you know where we might go next?'

'I have no idea. A lot will depend on whatever James has discovered about Henry Austen. I sent him a note yesterday from Basingstoke asking him to find out what he can.' A thought occurred to her. 'Oh, if you are offered a portrait commission please do not turn it down on my account. There is really no hurry in what I'm doing. It's really just an excuse to have a break from the theatre and spend time with you. Jane Austen is dead. It's not as if we have to complete our inquiries while she is ailing but still alive.'

'Bless you,' Elizabeth said. 'I really can't afford to turn down any work, no matter how minor. Unfortunately, I don't think another commission is likely in the near future. I might even take up landscape painting. I find it much more satisfying than having to make ugly men look handsome and miserable women look happy.'

Laughing, the two women embraced and parted, taking separate hackneys, Elizabeth to her studio in Chelsea, Sarah to her home in Portman Place.

***

James and her father had just started dinner when she arrived at Portman Place. She joined them, and during the meal brought them up to date with her inquiries. When she'd finished, her father said, 'It certainly sounds all rather weird. Henry Austen has gone from being her enthusiastic agent, doing deals for her with publishers, to denying that she had any interest in publishing her writing. There has to be an explanation.'

Sarah nodded. To James she said, 'Did you receive my note from Basingstoke?'

'I did. And I acted on it straight away.' He grinned. 'I put young Jack Godwin on to it. He's our best reporter and worth his weight in gold. I swear he's got ferret blood in his veins. And he's always so keen.'

Matthew Kedron laughed. 'You want to be careful, James. He's got his eye on your job.'

'I'll gladly give him the *Weekly Police News*, sir. He could edit that in his sleep. I'd much prefer to spend more time on *The Inquirer*.'

'And you shall, my boy,' Matthew said. 'Godwin will be ready to take on the *Weekly Police News* next year. Then you can devote all your time to *The Inquirer*. I've been thinking about starting something new. A magazine for reasonably educated women. There are going to be a lot more of them before long. You mark my words.'

'Don't delay too long, Father,' Sarah said. 'My article on Jane Austen could be in the first issue.'

James said, 'It won't be long before there will be a demand for specialist periodicals. It's a market we need to keep our eyes on.'

James Brewster had worked for Matthew for over two years. He'd launched the *Weekly Police News* and also helped by editing *The Inquirer*. The attempt at a single-sheet daily paper had been a mistake—the competition was just too great with over thirty daily papers in the capital. Matthew had discontinued it before it lost too much money. Now the business consisted of only the *Weekly Police News* and the *Monthly Inquirer*. The two publications were both profitable, benefiting not only from increasing sales but also abundant advertising.

Matthew already looked on James as a possible heir. At one time, he'd thought Sarah might be interested in marrying James, and then managing the business with him, but recent developments in her private life and her continued success as a playwright made that very unlikely.

Taking a folded piece of paper out of his coat pocket, James handed it to Sarah. 'This is Godwin's report. He also discovered an address for James Tilson, the main partner in Henry Austen's London bank until the collapse, and he has provisionally arranged for you and I to meet with him.'

Sarah quickly skimmed the report. Henry Austen's first entry into banking had been in Alton, little more than a large village, near Steventon. There he had gone into business with a Mr Gray, a prosperous local grocer. Within a few months, in spite of his total lack of experience of banking, he had branched out with new partners, Messrs Blunt and Louch, in Petersfield. Almost immediately, he had opened a third bank. This time in Henrietta Street in Covent Garden. Here he had two different partners, Messrs Maunde and Tilson. In 1815 all three banks failed. The partners lost their investments, as did several members of the Austen family, some of whom had put in a great deal of money. Most of the banks' business had been with government contractors of one kind another, but especially with suppliers of various goods and services to the military. The failure of the banks had to some extent been due to the downturn in the economy after the war, and the huge government debt that had resulted in substantial reductions in expenditure. It was more likely, though, the report suggested, that the banks had failed mainly due to rapid expansion and insufficient capital.

'Now he is just a curate in a small parish,' James observed. 'When all else fails, there is always the church as a refuge.'

'This is all very interesting,' Sarah said. 'Do thank Godwin for me. As you say, he is a treasure.'

'We are meeting Mr Tilson at the Chapter Coffee House tomorrow morning at ten,' James said.

'How did you know that's what I would have asked you to do?' Sarah smiled, but her voice carried a slight edge.

James ignored it. He was used to her and took her sensitivity for granted. 'Oh, it wasn't necessary to be a mind reader. He's the most obvious person to meet in London if you want to find out more about Henry Austen's life here. They were partners for more than ten years. We already know Henry acted as his sister's agent. It's likely that he was involved in her life in other ways. James Tilson would probably know if he was.'

'I have already decided,' Sarah said, 'that if I am to understand Jane Austen and her life, I need to find out as much as I can about her family and her relationships with them all. Not only does Henry's behaviour make one curious and want to know more, but her sister-in-law, Mary Austen, married to James, the eldest brother, made a significant remark. She told me that she would be pleased to talk to me about Jane, and in her words, "*if only to put the record straight.*"'

'Well! Well! The plot does thicken. That suggests there is a record that needs attention,' James said, and then added, 'I have arranged that you and I meet Mr Tilson together as I think that more appropriate than for you to meet him alone. There will be nothing unusual in me, a magazine editor, wanting his story. And if he is now short of money, I can offer payment. He would find it difficult to accept an offer of payment from a woman.' He laughed. 'Military pride and all that.'

'Sounds very good, James, thank you.' Sarah yawned and stood up. 'But now I must ask you both to excuse me. I have had a long and busy day. I need my bed.' She bent to kiss her father on the forehead, patted James's shoulder as if to say, 'I'm pleased' and then retired to her room.

Chapter Thirteen

When Sarah and James entered the coffee house, James asked a servant if there was a Mr Tilson waiting to see them. The servant nodded, and they followed him to a table in the far corner of the establishment. There, a strikingly handsome middle-aged, military-looking man, smartly dressed in a quality frock coat that now showed its age, watched their approach. As soon as he was sure they were coming to meet him, he stood up.

'James Tilson at your service. This is an unexpected pleasure, Miss Kedron,' he said, bowing low. As a keen theatregoer, he recognised her from her days on the stage. 'I have followed your career with interest.' He held out his hand to James. 'And you must be Mr Brewster. Good day to you, sir.'

After taking their seats, James explained why Sarah had accompanied him to the meeting. 'Miss Kedron, who is the daughter of the proprietor of *The Inquirer*, is the publication's theatre critic and contributes occasional fiction reviews. She is planning an important series on women novelists of the Regency. Jane Austen is her choice for the first article.'

'An excellent choice, if I may say so. Jane Austen was a most unusual woman. She will be remembered and read long after her contemporaries are forgotten.'

'I'm glad you approve,' Sarah said, smiling. 'I hope you can tell me something about her as a person.'

Sarah launched into her opening remarks. In her mind she had carefully prepared what she wanted to say. She hoped to be able to steer the conversation where she wanted it to go as though she were scripting a play. She was soon relieved to discover that she had no problems with Mr Tilson. He wanted to impress her, and the information she needed flowed from him in a torrent.

'I recently had the pleasure, Mr Tilson,' she said, 'of meeting your former business partner, Mr Henry Austen.'

Tilson's face clouded. 'At one time much more than that. He was my closest friend.'

'But no longer?'

'Few partnerships—or friendships, come to that—can survive what we have been through. We had so much and then suddenly we had nothing.'

'Had you known one another long?' James asked.

'About fifteen years. We both joined the Oxford Militia at the same time and rose to the rank of captain. He was still a single man. Then in 1797, I think it was, he married his cousin, the widow of the Compte de Feuillide who was tragically guillotined in Paris three years before with his estates in France being confiscated. But Eliza, who expected to be referred to and addressed as the Countess, had money of her own, and some of her husband's assets were transferred to England before the revolution took hold and madness ruled France. Henry had little money of his own. His officer's pay went nowhere, but his wife's income remedied his situation. As young officers about town with beautiful wives, we lived a very full social life and Eliza's title—though perhaps of somewhat doubtful provenance—as well as her great charm and intelligence, ensured that we were able to mix with appropriate people.'

It occurred to James that Tilson and Henry Austen had probably persuaded some of these 'appropriate people' to invest in their bank. Since its collapse, they would no longer be welcome at their investors' dinners and soirées.

'I was not aware that Henry Austen was married,' Sarah said.

'Widowed. Eliza died in 1813. Her only son, Hastings, whom she had with the Compte, died young. He was not a normal child. Some inherited condition.'

'Hastings is an unusual Christian name,' James said.

Tilson leant forward. 'Thereby hangs a tale.'

And, James thought, *wild horses and all the king's men won't prevent you from telling it.* He felt Tilson was trying hard not to reveal how badly let down he felt by the bankruptcy and Henry Austen's role in it. In self-defence he needed to blame the situation largely on his ex-partner. If there were scandal to be had about Henry, he would not hesitate to pass it on.

'Eliza was Henry's first cousin,' Tilson continued, 'the only child of his aunt Philadelphia, his father's sister. In 1753 or thereabouts, Philadelphia Austen sailed to India hoping to snare a husband.'

'The fishing fleet,' Sarah said, smiling. 'Shiploads of rather plain young women from good but financially straightened families. Their only hope of making anything like a good marriage, or in some cases a marriage of any kind, was to go to India where there were scores of young men of good fortune faced with a serious shortage of white women.'

'Precisely,' Tilson said, smiling.

'What happened to the girls who didn't find a husband?' James asked.

Sarah grinned wickedly. 'They were returned empty.'

A little embarrassed by Sarah's remark, James said to Tilson, 'But Philadelphia was fortunate?'

'Yes. Within a few weeks she married Mr Tysoe Hancock. He had a good position with prospects with the East India Company. The couple moved in the right social circles, but their marriage went without issue, until that is, they met and became friendly with Mr Warren Hastings.'

'Ah!' James said, 'that's a name to conjure with. He became Governor of Bengal and only a few years ago was acquitted of corruption after one of the longest trials in British history.'

'A mischief monger by the name of Jenny Strachey started a rumour,' Tilson continued, keeping his voice so low that James and Sarah had to lean forward to hear him above the noise in the coffee house, 'that Eliza was not Hancock's child but was fathered by Warren Hastings. Whether there is any foundation in this rumour, we will never know, but Tysoe Hancock heard the rumour himself and wrote to his wife warning her about Mrs Strachey's attempts to estrange her from society. Thus, he accepted paternity, but to stop the tongues wagging, Tysoe and Philadelphia appointed Warren Hastings as Eliza's official godfather. This enabled Warren Hastings to settle a considerable sum on her as well as send her further sums throughout her life. When Eliza gave birth to a child of her own, she christened him Hastings in honour of his ... of his godfather grandparent, I suppose.'

'That's an amazing story,' Sarah said. 'Do you think Henry Austen knew of this rumour?'

'If he did, it did not worry him, nor apparently, was it any great concern to Tysoe Hancock.'

James said, 'If the only evidence in support of the rumour is that Warren Hastings settled substantial sums of money on Eliza, then in legal terms, the case would fail. Warren Hastings has a reputation for extravagance and generosity. He gives large sums of money to many people. As far as is known, he didn't sire them all, if any of them.'

'Tell me about Eliza,' Sarah said, wanting to steer the conversation to Jane Austen. 'Presumably she knew Jane, Henry's sister.'

'More than just knew her. She became young Jane Austen's mentor. She was at least ten years older than her cousin, well educated—she had been to a girls' seminary in France and was, of course, bi-lingual—she adored the theatre and detected in Jane a budding writer.'

'How?'

'Eliza frequently visited Steventon when the family lived there. They were mad about amateur theatricals. The rector even allowed Henry and his brother James to turn one of the barns into a small theatre. The whole family, with some local friends, put on plays. James often wrote prologues or epilogues for them. Apparently, Jane, even as a child—she would have been about fourteen—wrote little plays, parodies of the kinds of plays she had seen, or they put on. Burlesques, I suppose. She also wrote what she called novels, but they were really just absurd plot outlines. Short satires. She was very precocious and grown-up for her age, but critical of the way adults behaved, especially the socially ambitious and pretentious middle class. Eliza encouraged her to write, and when Jane visited them in London, Eliza took her to the theatre and generally became her mentor.'

'And taught her the necessary social skills, no doubt,' Sarah said.

'Not at all. Jane had no idea how to behave in a socially acceptable way.' Tilson gave the impression of being adamant on this topic. 'She either remained aloof and silent or spoke out when it would have been better if she had kept her opinions to herself. She had an acid tongue, and her wit, though clever enough, was usually scathing and hurtful. She seemed to take pride and pleasure in putting people down. When she had selected her target, she was merciless. Not a pleasant characteristic in a young woman.'

'Did Eliza encourage this?' Sarah asked, a little incredulously.

'In my presence, she did not encourage it, but she certainly made no attempt to put a stop to it.'

'I assume you did not like Jane?' James said.

'My wife, Frances, detested her. If it were not for our pleasure in Eliza's company, we would have absented ourselves when Jane came to visit.'

'Was that often?'

'Several times a year, usually. I was amazed at the amount of time, not to say money, that the family spent in travelling. Jane's excuse for her visits to London was that she had to read the proofs of her novels. She would shut herself away in Henry's lodgings for days at a time. She was very dedicated to her writing and was always complaining about her publisher.'

'Because?' James said.

'Oh, she thought they did not pay her well, or they were too slow bringing her books out. Henry sold the copyright in her first book for ten pounds and the publisher never got around to publishing it.'

Sarah said, 'She had good cause to complain. That's disgraceful.'

'Henry felt awfully bad about it. He thought he'd let her down. He made up for his mistake by accepting responsibility for the costs of publication of *Sense and Sensibility* which Egerton published on commission. Fortunately, the book made a profit.

Jane now had evidence that it would not be impossible for her to become financially independent of her family. From then, books seemed to pour from her.'

'Was work on her proofs all she did when she came to London?' Sarah asked.

'No, no. While Eliza was alive, they went everywhere together, especially to the theatre. Henry, of course, was keen on the theatre. He should have been an actor not a banker. Had Eliza not had a substantial income from Warren Hastings' various gifts, she would probably have gone on the stage.'

'And soon found a protector, no doubt,' James observed.

Tilson nodded. 'Quite possibly. She had all the skills of a courtesan, I'm sure. But nothing about Eliza is straight-forward. Henry confided in me that he was not her first choice as a husband. She had turned him down twice. She was after his brother, James, but he wasn't interested.'

'Do you think,' Sarah said, wanting to bring the conversation back to Jane again, 'that Eliza helped Jane with her writing?'

'She certainly encouraged it, but more than that, I have no knowledge. I rather doubt if Jane needed any encouragement. She gave the impression of being wholly dedicated to it. Nothing else was of any importance.'

'No interest in marriage?'

'None whatsoever. I think she might have been something of a flirt when she was younger, but by the time I came to know her, she showed no interest in men. Quite simply, she lived for her work. She considered it to be her profession.'

'That's all very interesting,' Sarah said. 'Certainly, towards the end of her life she must have spent hours every day on her writing. Her six novels were published within six years.'

'You mentioned that she travelled a great deal to visit relatives. Do you know to which relative she visited most often?' James asked.

'I can't be sure, but I think it was to another brother, Edward. Jane had six brothers, not five as some members of the family insist. Her father's second son, George, was born with an impediment. He was fostered out as a baby and is never spoken of. Edward inherited Godmersham Park in Kent. But he has ceased to be an ordinary Austen. He now calls himself Austen Knight.'

'I don't understand.'

'As a child, he was favoured by his father's relatives, Thomas Knight and his wife, Catherine. I know little about them except that they were very wealthy but childless, so they took a fancy to the boy when he was twelve. Thomas Knight made Edward his beneficiary, and when Catherine Knight died in 1812, she requested in her will that Edward adopt the surname Knight.'

'Did Jane travel alone to Godmersham Park?'

'I think occasionally with her mother, but usually with her sister, Cassandra. They made a strange pair. They were obviously devoted to one another, but Cassandra was totally different in character and personality. She never said anything to anyone that could give offence. It was almost as if she were trying to make up for her sister's inappropriate behaviour by being especially pleasant to everyone. She was very much the clergyman's daughter and, I am sure, very devout. Pious even and probably a little narrow-minded, even bigoted. I know she disapproved strongly of Eliza and of her influence on Jane.'

'But Eliza was the star in the Austen firmament,' James said.

'Very much so. But many in the family did not approve of her. She was an extraordinary woman. A bit rackety and a terrible flirt, but, I think, harmless. Though she had very unorthodox views about marriage—she didn't believe in it.'

'But she married twice nevertheless,' Sarah said.

'That's true. You asked just now if Eliza had any role in Jane's writing. Perhaps she did. There's a long passage in one of her books that my wife read to me. I can't remember which one. It was a diatribe against marriage. It could be Eliza talking. I always thought, though, that she and Henry were happy together. They enjoyed the same things, the same kind of life. I have to admit, though, that Henry is a little strange.

He's also a bit of a cold fish. You only realise it when you get to know him well. He is always charming and good company, but he is one of those people who does not have a fixed personality. They take on the colouring, so to speak, of the environment in which they happen to be.'

'Like so many actors I know.' Sarah laughed. 'I sometimes wonder who they really are when they are not playing a part. Perhaps they are no one. Sans character. Sans personality.'

'I am sure Henry will perform the role of a country parson very effectively,' James Tilson said. His change in tone revealed a deep-rooted bitterness. 'He convinced so many investors that he was a competent and reliable banker. No doubt he will be able to convince his parishioners that he is a devout man of God.'

'Did Jane have friends in London who could be willing to talk about her?' Sarah asked.

'None that I know of. Acquaintances, no more. She was a complex and, I believe, far from happy woman. She expected instant success as an author, but she died before she really achieved it. She remained dependent on her family for money and resented this. She became an author, I believe, because authorship is one of the few ways that an educated woman can earn a living. The choice of occupation for a middle-class woman who does not wish to marry or cannot attract a suitable husband is really limited to becoming a governess or a teacher of some kind. It is not a happy state in which to be.'

'In the brief biography that Henry published together with *Northanger Abbey* and *Persuasion*,' Sarah said, 'Henry wrote that Jane had no interest in fame or fortune, and that she even insisted on being an anonymous author of the four titles published in her lifetime.'

'That statement amazes me. I cannot explain it. I can assume only that Henry has his reason for making it.' Mr Tilson took his watch out of his pocket, glanced at the time and returned the watch to his pocket. 'It has been a great pleasure meeting you. I must now leave you as I have an appointment.' He stood.

Sarah offered her hand, and as he bent to kiss it, she said, 'We are greatly obliged to you for your time and most useful information.'

James stood. The men bowed to one another and Tilson hurried away.

'Well!' Sarah exclaimed as Tilson left the coffee house, 'all that needs a lot of taking in and sorting out. One thing is immediately obvious.'

'And that is?'

'Next stop, Godmersham. But first, I'll see John Murray, the publisher, and then make my way to Kent.'

Chapter Fourteen

When Sarah gave her card to the clerk in the front office of Murray's premises and he had taken it into his employer, barely half a minute passed before Murray himself welcomed her and ushered her into his comfortable, book-lined room at the rear of the building.

John Murray, publisher, quickly reminded Sarah that he was well-acquainted with her father, Matthew Kedron. 'This is an unexpected pleasure, Miss Kedron. I trust your father is in excellent health.'

'He is, thank you.'

Murray indicated that she should sit in one of the two high-backed armchairs, one each side of a small table, and said, 'May I offer you refreshment?'

'Thank you, but no. I have just left the Chapter Coffee House.'

Murray smiled. 'I am hoping,' he said, 'that the purpose of your visit is to offer me the honour of publishing your plays. Let me say immediately that I shall be delighted to become your publisher.'

Sarah laughed. 'Well, Mr Murray, I had no such intention until a few seconds ago, but that is certainly something we can discuss while I'm here, but for the present, I have another matter in mind.' She explained her interest in his author, Jane Austen, concluding, 'I am wondering, among other things, why she left Thomas Egerton and came to you.'

'Oh, I think there were two reasons. Jane Austen was a most ambitious lady. She was determined to do what was best for her writing. I publish Lord Byron and I co-publish Sir Walter Scott. I am sure Miss Austen desired to be included in that company. My books are also more attractively produced than Egerton's, a good publisher though he is. He does his best for his authors.'

'Perhaps you also offered her better terms,' Sarah said.

'Negotiations were, shall we say, protracted? Mr Henry Austen came to me at first, but he was taken ill and Miss Austen herself took over. Finally, after the poor woman's tragically early death, her sister, Miss Cassandra Austen completed the negotiations.'

'A somewhat fraught situation.'

'Initially I offered Jane Austen an outright sum for three of her copyrights. *Sense and Sensibility*, *Mansfield Park* and the unpublished novel, *Emma*—possibly her masterpiece. But it became clear that she was not interested in selling her copyrights for anything like a reasonable sum. She had learnt from bitter experience that if your work has commercial potential, the best arrangement for an author is for her books to be published on a commission basis.'

'So she still owned the copyright in three books, but not in all. That means that she had sold the copyright on *Pride and Prejudice*.'

'Yes. Unless Egerton is prepared to sell it, he can publish as many editions of it as he wishes, without further payment to Miss Austen's estate, until his interest in the copyright expires. I think that is in about ten years' time.'

'You have not only published *Emma* but also two more titles, *Northanger Abbey* and *Persuasion*. All on commission?'

'Unfortunately, yes. I didn't really want *Northanger Abbey*. It is by far her weakest book. But I wanted *Mansfield Park*, and *Persuasion*. Miss Cassandra Austen, who inherited her sister's estate and became her executor, was determined that all three of her sister's last books should be published. Apparently, the family had bought back the copyright for *Northanger Abbey* from Messrs Cadell who had been sitting on the unpublished manuscript for years.'

Sarah made a quick calculation in her head. 'So in fact, you have access to the whole of Jane Austen's output, except for *Pride and Prejudice*. But only on a commission basis.'

'All of it that is known—or that Cassandra Austen thinks is fit to print.'

Sarah thought this an interesting comment. It implied that Cassandra had given John Murray the impression that she was prepared to act as a kind of censor of her sister's work. 'Are you aware of any unfinished manuscripts?' she asked.

'I know only that Jane Austen continued writing almost until the day of her death. And that she had started two further novels but managed only a few chapters for each. She was totally committed to her work. I cannot help thinking that she spent her last days in a writing frenzy, desperately trying to get down on paper ideas that were racing around in her head.'

'But according to her brother, she had no interest in fame or fortune. So what drove her?'

John Murray shrugged. 'I cannot explain that statement of Mr Austen's in his memorial piece. It does not conform in any way to my opinion of the Jane Austen I met.'

'Even though she required that *Emma* be published anonymously?'

'I assumed that this was at the insistence of one of her family; Miss Cassandra Austen, or the mother, perhaps.'

'Forgive me for pressing the point, Mr Murray, but Jane Austen was barely dead in her grave before her sister allowed you to publish those two remaining books without the condition that they should be published anonymously.'

'That is true. Perhaps that was because I explained the opportunity of benefiting from better sales of her new titles if we revealed the identity of the author.' He smiled. 'I think Miss Cassandra Austen took into consideration the possibility of greater commercial success.'

'The failure of Mr Austen's bank has presumably affected the Austen family's fortunes,' Sarah said.

But if the decision to publish *Emma* anonymously had been Jane's alone, she thought, it still needed explanation. By the date she offered *Emma* for publication, Henry's bank had already failed. He would no longer be a source of financial help. Sarah could not understand why an author who was in every other way a committed professional and determined to earn as much money from her writing as possible, refused to be identified as the author of the first four novels while she was still alive. She wondered if the dedication in *Emma* to the Prince Regent had something to do with it.

'How did Jane Austen feel about being asked to dedicate a book to the Prince Regent?' she asked.

John Murray lapsed into his native dialect in his response. 'Aye, she didna wanta do it. The lassie loathed the man. And who could blame her?'

'What persuaded her?'

'I explained that royal approval, even from such a creature as the Prince Regent could be worth its weight in gold. He might head up a subscription list to a future book ensuring a good profit.'

'And did it?'

'We heard nothing from him. I sent an expensive, specially bound copy to Carlton House but did not receive even an acknowledgement of its receipt. I fear the brevity of the dedication and total absence of flattery caused offence.'

Sarah nodded to indicate her understanding. Bringing the discussion to an end, she observed, 'This has been most interesting, Mr Murray. It will be a great pity if the family finds it difficult to keep all six titles in print.'

'The sales are fortunately likely to generate more income than the costs of production. And I believe will continue to do so for many years to come.' He smiled. 'Jane Austen knew what she was doing.'

'One last question. A personal one. Did you like her?'

John Murray stroked his chin thoughtfully. Had this question been asked by anyone except Sarah, he would have avoided an answer. As it was, he decided to be frank with her. 'I tried to, but she had a very abrupt manner, almost rude. She pestered me continually to get her books out faster. I know now, of course, that she was dying and determined to get her books finished and, if possible, published before she died. Authors are like fond parents, Miss Kedron. They often look upon their books as if they are their children. I know Jane Austen did.'

Sarah smiled. 'Mr Murray, you have been most helpful. I am deeply obliged to you.'

'It has been my pleasure, Miss Kedron. Perhaps now we may discuss the publication of your plays?'

And this they did. John Murray Ltd was not even given an opportunity to make an offer for the copyrights. Sarah had learnt that the best arrangement for an author was for the publisher to publish the work on commission.

Chapter Fifteen

Sarah took a hackney to her father's office to collect any letters that had arrived for her before planning her next move in the Jane Austen investigation. She had several options, and all involved journeys out of London. However, she had to wait until she received a reply from the Lord Chamberlain's office before leaving the city for any length of time. If changes were required to her play, they had to be made immediately.

On her arrival at the office, the chief clerk handed her an official-looking package from Carlton House. With some trepidation she tore open the wrapping. Her play had been returned. This could mean it had been rejected. She flipped through the script looking for a covering letter. Eventually, she found it between the section which contained most of the additional scenes. To her immense relief, it was short and to the point. It informed her that the Lord Chamberlain was pleased to advise her that the script could be performed in appropriately licensed theatres without changes. She sighed with relief. This provided a possibility, perhaps even a probability, that Mr Kean would be willing to perform the title role in the play in the forthcoming season. She decided to take the script to the theatre and then continue to Elizabeth's studio. They would decide together to whom or to where they should visit next. Delaying only to write and send a 'Thank you' letter to Revd J.S. Clarke, the Prince Regent's librarian, she took another hackney to the theatre. There, the manager, Samuel Arnold, expressed his pleasure in having her play available for production. While skimming through the additions, he expressed the opinion that she had nothing about which to worry. He felt confident that the amended script would delight Mr Kean as it now provided opportunities for him to dominate the play. Mr Arnold told Sarah that he would instruct the prompter to organise printing copies of the play as soon as Kean had agreed to perform in it. Sarah was now able to concentrate on the next stage of her investigation into the life of Jane Austen.

Over a light lunch at the Crossed Keys tavern in Cheyne Walk where Elizabeth had her studio apartment, the two friends planned their next journey.

'We shall probably need to talk to more people,' Sarah said, 'but at present, there are three on whom we should concentrate. The most promising is Mary Austen, the Reverend James Austen's wife at Steventon. Remember, she said she would "put the record straight," which I find most intriguing. Then we have Cassandra Austen and her mother, who live together at Chawton, which is not all that far from Steventon. I am sure that Cassandra knows more about Jane than anyone else, but I fear she may refuse to even speak to me. It depends on what, if anything, Henry Austen has said to her about us. Though I have a suspicion that even if she agrees to see us, she will not say a word in criticism of her sister.'

'Wasn't there a younger brother at the funeral?' Elizabeth asked.

'Yes. Frances or Frank as the family call him. He's a naval officer living in Portsmouth, presumably awaiting a ship. I've left a note for James Brewster asking him if one of his journalists can find out some information about him.'

'Wait,' Elizabeth said. 'If it is the same Francis Austen, I invited him for a portrait sitting after his name appeared in *The Times*. Wasn't he made a Companion of the Bath some five years ago?'

Sarah smiled. 'In that case, he shouldn't be too difficult to find. It'll be just a question of discreetly asking around and consulting the Navy List. Finally, there's Edward Austen who received a substantial inheritance from the Knight family and lives in some style, I believe, at Godmersham Park in Kent. What is important, Lizzy, is the order in which we meet these people. What each of them tells us, or doesn't tell us, can affect whom we see next and how we approach them.'

Elizabeth remained silent for a few moments, and then she said, 'We're assuming, aren't we, that the family, or at least some members of it, are trying to hide something about Jane. Something she was, or something she did.'

'Or both. Exactly.'

'Then it seems that Cassandra is the least likely to be honest with us, even, as you say, to the extent of refusing to talk to us.'

'I think you could be right.'

'Then perhaps we should put her towards the end of our list. By then we should know enough to be able to judge whether there is something about her sister that Cassandra doesn't want to be known.'

'That makes sense, my dear. So it's between Edward and Frank.'

Elizabeth furrowed her brow while she considered, and after a moment, she said, 'Then I would choose Edward. Francis or Frank has probably been at sea for most of Jane's writing life. He will know only what his family chose to reveal in letters.'

Sarah agreed. 'Then Godmersham it is. If it's convenient for you, we'll leave for Kent tomorrow. In the meantime, I'll find out from which inn the coach to Godmersham departs, and where we should stay when we get there. I'll dine this evening with my father and James and tell them what we've discovered so far. They might have useful suggestions. Now tell me what you have been doing.'

Elizabeth excitedly told Sarah that she had been commissioned to do a family portrait of a successful diamond merchant in Hatton Garden. The first sitting would take place as soon as the merchant could get his family together: his wife, two sons at boarding school and a married daughter with the babe in arms. They had a house on the river at Putney, and he was hoping for an alfresco setting, though much depended on the weather. She thought the sitting would be at least a couple of weeks away, so nothing prevented her from spending a few days in Kent, and she would take her easel and paints as before.

'Spending time with you in the country, dearest,' she said, taking Sarah's hand, 'is changing my life, you know. I've been working up the sketches I made of the Steventon church and rectory. I've discovered that I enjoy painting buildings as much as I enjoy doing portraits. With all these huge country houses being built everywhere by the new wealthy merchant class and factory owners, there's a lot of work for artists who they think will do justice to their client's proudest possession.'

Sarah laughed. 'After their wives, Lizzy.'

'Oh no. House and garden first, then the male heir if there is one, then the wife. In many cases I think they will exclude the wife if they can. Especially if she is either fat and ugly or so worn out with child-bearing that she destroys the impression of affluence. It's his mistress he would have in the picture if he could. Men!'

'Men!' Sarah repeated, and laughing, the two women parted for the day.

Chapter Sixteen

Sarah discovered that the small village of
Godmersham was an equidistance of about six miles
between Canterbury and Ashford, both of which
were about sixty miles from London. Coaches
destined for or passing through both places came
frequently, but Canterbury was by far the most
interesting architecturally, so she decided they would
travel there by coach and stay at one of the many inns
or hotels.

Sarah reasoned that even if the visit to
Godmersham Park turned out to be a waste of time,
Elizabeth would be able to sketch and even paint
scenes of interest in this part of Kent notable for its
natural beauty. As they had done in Basingstoke, they

would hire horses or a simple gig to take them from the city to Godmersham. They would turn it into another short holiday together.

She considered whether to write in advance to request a meeting but decided against this. A letter could be ignored—which could be in itself a refusal—or replied to with a polite excuse. If, as at Steventon, they just turned up, conventional middle-class politeness would not allow them to be abruptly turned away. They would stand a good chance of at least some conversation with Edward Austen Knight who might have something of interest to say about his sister.

Accordingly, Sarah sent a messenger to book two inside seats on the next morning's first coach to Canterbury and then to deliver a note asking Elizabeth to meet her at eight-thirty at The White Horse Inn, Fetter Lane, from where the coach would depart.

They had a fine day for their eight-hour journey, and after resting in their hotel in Canterbury, they strolled around the attractive cathedral city before taking a light supper and retiring early. After breakfast the next morning, Sarah hired a gig to take them to Godmersham Park. So far, the expedition had been sufficiently pleasant not to turn out to be a waste of time even if Edward Austen had nothing of interest to tell them.

As they approached Godmersham Park, Sarah reined in the horse and the gig came to a halt outside the large iron gates through which they could see the house at the end of a long drive.

'Good Gracious,' Elizabeth exclaimed. 'Just look at the size of it!'

Laughing, Sarah said, 'It's certainly not what I expected.'

The house was not in any way an ordinary country dwelling but rather a vast mansion, superbly sited in parkland where deer grazed, and swans moved gently about on a large ornamental lake. At a glance, the house consisted of a central two-storey building with what appeared to be eight front bedrooms in the second storey. A two-storey annexe or wing, each of which was the size of a substantial dwelling, was attached to each side of this main building. Doubtless, at the rear of the main building would be many outhouses and even cottages. Godmersham Park was fit to be the home of a duke.

Sarah knew nothing about the Knight family. Obviously, however, if their residence was anything to go by, they were undeniably wealthy. Perhaps even aristocrats with a distinguished history. The house, which looked fairly recent, perhaps mid-period Georgian, would need at least a score of inside servants, and probably half-a-dozen more employees of one kind and another worked in the park and gardens. Sarah could not help wondering where the money came from to support such luxury, and she suspected that the initial wealth had come from trafficking in slaves, which would be the same as for many other recently built large country houses.

In the previous century, it had been commonplace for successful merchants, industrialists and bankers—and even those at the top of the social tree—to invest in the slave ships carrying their human cargo from Africa to plantations in the West Indies and elsewhere. Although British slave-carrying ships no longer existed, the ownership of slaves was still legal in the colonies. Plantations were highly profitable as slaves costing a one-off payment of less than an English domestic servant's annual wage worked them.

It occurred to Sarah that Godmersham Park might have been the inspiration for Jane Austen's novel *Mansfield Park*, in which she hinted that the Bertram family owed their wealth to slave labour on their estate in Antigua. She could not help wondering what other dark matters a careful reading of Austen's novels might reveal. If there were such, then this was a possible explanation for Jane—or her family—not wanting their name to be associated with her books in case they were interpreted as a vehicle for expressing radical opinions. It had to be borne in mind that the family had close connections with the Anglican Church, a bastion of conservatism and middle-class morality. Jane's father had been a rector, two of her brothers had taken holy orders, and she was buried in Winchester Cathedral.

'I must draw this wonderful place,' Elizabeth exclaimed.

'Perhaps we could make a meeting with Edward Austen more likely by concentrating on the illustrations you will be providing for my article,' Sarah said. 'It might make him less suspicious of what I might write about Jane.'

'I'm happy with that, dearest,' Elizabeth said. 'Let's go in. I can't wait to start.'

As Sarah turned the horse to face the house, a lodge-keeper, who had been awaiting developments, emerged from the lodge and swung open the huge gates. He touched his forelock in acknowledgement of Sarah's smile, then closed the gates behind the gig as it proceeded up the drive to the house. By the time they reached the steps, their approach had been noticed inside the house and a footman waited to attend to them.

Both women, being fashionably dressed, were clearly of an acceptable class. They thought it would be assumed they were making a social call and would leave cards if no one of importance was at home to receive them. They were in luck, however. While a stable lad held the horse's reins to keep the gig steady, a footman took their cards and immediately escorted them into a drawing room. Within a minute, the butler advised them that Mr Edward Austen Knight would receive them shortly.

'It's a good thing we know how to behave, Lizzy,' Sarah whispered, 'and that I have access to the Drury Lane wardrobe. If we'd been wearing our usual clothes, we would have been sent round the back.'

While waiting, they walked to the floor-to-ceiling French windows and stared out at the park.

'One family has all this,' Elizabeth said. 'It can't be right. I mean, what have they done to deserve it?'

'Perhaps we'll find out,' Sarah said, 'though I doubt whether Mr Edward Austen Knight has contributed much. He came late to the Knight family wealth.'

A few moments later, Edward entered the room. He wore riding clothes and had presumably been inspecting his estate. He held their cards in his hand.

'Which of you is the playwright and critic and which the artist?' he asked with a smile. 'I need to know to whom I need to ask the appropriate questions.'

'I am the playwright and critic, Mr Austen Knight. My father is the proprietor of the *Monthly Inquirer.*'

'An interesting journal. I rarely agree with most of it, but no one can deny the quality of the writing.' He indicated for the women to be seated. 'How may I be of assistance to you? Or is this a social call to inform me that you have moved into the district?'

Sarah explained the purpose of their visit, stressing, as she and Elizabeth had agreed, the importance of the illustrations. Edward listened with genuine interest. He seemed an amiable man with a pleasant, open face and a warm smile. He lacked the good looks of his brother, Henry, though he appeared to be a great deal healthier and considerably stouter. His manner and appearance spoke a lot of the county squire.

When Sarah had finished her explanation for their visit, he turned to Elizabeth and said, 'Miss Stockton, you will be most welcome to make any drawings you wish of the house and park. As for details of my late sister's life, Miss Kedron, I will ask my eldest daughter, Fanny, to do her best to answer your questions. She was her Aunt Jane's favourite niece, and they wrote to each other frequently. Jane also visited from time to time, and we regularly visit Chawton where I have an estate. I will send Fanny to you. And now if you will excuse me, I must return to the task in which I was engaged before your arrival.' He smiled, bowed and left the room.

'I'll start sketching,' Elizabeth said, 'and leave you to talk to Fanny.'

'That'll be perfect, Lizzy. And would you ask that servant if he would take the gig to the stable? We may be here some time, and the horse could do with a drink and might even get a rub down.'

Elizabeth nodded and left the room to fetch her pad and sketching pencil from the gig. Sarah adjusted her thoughts. Her approach to Fanny would depend on the girl's age.

Chapter Seventeen

Sarah did not have to wait long before Fanny arrived. However, Fanny Austen Knight was not a girl but a tall, slim woman in her mid-twenties with a rather hard and haughty expression. Sarah formed the impression that Fanny was self-confident and would be determined to take charge of the conversation. She did not offer Sarah her hand but invited her to resume her seat, clearly prepared to grant a few minutes of her time but not yet decided how to treat the visitor.

'Papa tells me you wish to question me about my Aunt Jane,' she said.

'You were her favourite niece, apparently, Miss Knight,' Sarah replied.

'Austen Knight,' Fanny said abruptly, then explained, 'My father changed the family name at the request of his late benefactress, Mrs Catherine Knight, in her will.' She smiled sweetly, but Sarah saw no warmth in it. 'As for Aunt Jane, in one of her last letters, she described me as inimitable, irresistible and the delight of her life. Yes,' she continued. 'She gave me advice concerning my writing and often wrote to me.'

Sarah nodded. 'And you to her, no doubt.'

'Not as often. We led very different lives.'

'In what way?'

'I lead a very busy social life,' Fanny replied. 'Our position in Kent society is very different from the Austen's in Hampshire. Since our mother died, I have been my father's hostess.' Having established her position, Fanny began to relax. 'Aunt Jane was really like an elder sister to me. I was able to talk to her about many things.' She managed another slight smile. 'Among other subjects, she liked to give me advice about love and marriage.'

'Was it good advice?'

'It was always worth hearing. I found her conversation amusing and often thought-provoking. She was strongly opposed to marrying without love.'

'Do you think that is why she never married?'

'Possibly. You must understand, Miss Kedron, that her writing was the most important thing in her life. Something in her made her want to write about the lives of the kinds of people about whom she knew so much. She understood their fears and worries. So much of what she wrote is concerned with money, of course, and social position. The men wanted to marry women with money. The women wanted to marry men with money, preferably from a good family. Marriages for love may be the ideal, but they are not what most marriages are, and she was very aware of this.'

Sarah smiled. 'And she waited for love. Money was not important.'

'It was very important, but she would not allow it to influence her attitude to marriage. She had no money of her own and no wealthy father to provide a dowry to take to a marriage. She was accustomed to having very little. Once she told me that when her father, the Reverend Austen, was alive and they lived at Steventon, her dress allowance was twenty pounds each year. Just twenty pounds. How could she have managed? Writing paper is also expensive, you know, and that is where she spent her money. That, with a few books and travel. She was an inveterate traveller and frequently visited relatives and family friends. She needed to meet people, I suppose, to get ideas for her books.'

'That's very understandable,' Sarah said. 'And I suppose some of the people she met she put in her books.'

'She liked to deny that she did, but I believe she did it quite often. Some of her characters could be our mutual acquaintances.'

'Did she have many friends?'

'No, on the contrary,' Fanny replied. 'Aunt Jane had very few friends. I would describe the people she mostly associated with as mere acquaintances or family. Certainly, no close men friends. Although I do not think she disliked men as such, but from a man's point of view, she was not an especially attractive woman. She dressed very drably in clothes more suited for an older woman, and she had a wicked tongue. I have witnessed her reducing a man to a speechless, blushing fool with a retort to something he said that annoyed her. She would not have been easy to live with.'

'Did she ever have a proposal of marriage?'

'I know of one from Mr Harris Bigg-Wither, but this was many years ago. He and his sisters were neighbours. They have a charming house, Manydown Hall, which is not far from Steventon. They often visited the Austens, and the Austens visited them. Apparently, when Aunt Jane was about twenty-six or twenty-seven, a somewhat younger Mr Bigg-Wither proposed during one of these visits. Anyway, she accepted him, then in the morning told him she'd changed her mind.'

'Do you know why?'

'Oh, I was just a child, but I can guess. Harris Bigg-Wither had a bad stutter and was not very clever. He came down from Oxford without a degree.'

'Did you ever meet him?' Sarah asked.

'Oh yes, during one of our visits to Steventon. I think Aunt Jane was rather selfish in turning him down. As his wife—he inherited the Manydown estate—she would have been able to ensure that her sister and mother had no financial worries. And Manydown Park is a lovely little place. Quite idyllic.'

'But she realised that she did not love him enough.'

'One has to think of one's family, Miss Kedron. Aunt Jane was kind to me, but she was very self-centred. There is another family rumour that she may have been attracted to a man she met when they were on holiday in the West Country. But nothing came of it.'

'Do you know who it was?'

'He is forever nameless. It was probably nothing. Just somebody she danced with more than once.' Then, laughing rather scornfully, Fanny said, 'She left me a lock of her hair and a bodkin in her will. I have no idea why she thought I would ever need a bodkin, so I gave it to my maid. I would have preferred nicely bound copies of her books.'

This wholly unnecessary and spiteful revelation made Sarah suspect that Fanny's intention in being so frank about Jane and her family's situation had an ulterior motive. It appeared a deliberate decision to distance herself, a Knight, from the Austens, the poor relations.

'Did she often visit here?' Sarah asked.

'Not so often. I think she felt out of place here. Her closest friend was our governess, Miss Anne Sharp. Whenever Aunt Jane visited, she spent most of her time with Miss Sharp. They had a lot in common and went on long walks together. Jane felt at ease with her, I suppose.'

'In what way?'

'If she couldn't make a living from her writing, I think Aunt Jane expected that she would probably end up as a governess like Miss Sharp. She felt sorry for her and sympathised with her situation.' A memory flashed into Fanny's mind. 'We had a hairdresser who came to do our hair. He was told to charge Aunt Jane less. Instead of being grateful that we understood her situation, she felt … oh, I don't know … insulted, perhaps. She was … What is the word? Touchy. Quick to take offence. Very different from her sister, Aunt Cassandra.'

Sarah wondered why the Knights risked offending Jane by allowing her to discover the arrangement. The extra expenditure for them would have been as nothing.

'Did your Aunt Cassandra often visit?' she asked.

'Oh, yes. When Mama died after giving birth to her last baby, there were eleven of us to look after. Aunt Cassandra came to live here for almost a year to help Papa with the family. There were nurses and governesses, of course, but they were not family.'

'Your Aunt Jane didn't come?'

Fanny replied, 'She wasn't really very interested in young children. And my mother had not liked her very much. It was Aunt Cassandra and Uncle Henry whom she always made welcome. Uncle Henry was always very charming and amusing. Aunt Cassandra went out of the way to be helpful. She is a saint. My mother was very fond of them both. And so was Papa, of course. He liked to shoot with Uncle Henry. He had been a captain in the militia.'

'And your Uncle Henry's wife, the Countess?'

'My mother did not want her in the house. She thought she would be a bad influence on me and on my sisters. She expected us to call her Countess, but never behaved like one. Her behaviour was outrageous, and the things she said are unrepeatable. At any social event she made a beeline for the most handsome or wealthiest man in the room. She was an unashamed flirt. I appreciate she has been dead at least five years, but she was a great embarrassment to Mama and Papa, and she wasn't even a real countess. It was derived from the worthless title awarded to her former husband.'

'Your Aunt Jane liked her, though, didn't she?'

'I think she was probably responsible for Aunt Jane's lack of good manners and many of her opinions,' Fanny replied. 'She was mad about the theatre, of course, and loved to act. She would have been at home among the theatricals. Whenever Aunt Jane visited London, she always took her to Drury Lane and the Lyceum. And she encouraged her to write. Aunt Jane told me that her first novel was largely inspired by Eliza. She was rather common, I'm afraid.'

'Oh? *Sense and Sensibility*?' This made no sense to Sarah. None of the characters in the novel was anything like what she had heard about the Countess Eliza de Feuillide.

'No. It was never published. I think Aunt Cassandra forbad her even to offer it to a publisher.' She laughed. 'Perhaps Aunt Eliza and Aunt Jane wrote it together. Just for fun, you know.'

'Do you know the title?'

'I don't think it has one. Anyway, Aunt Cassandra probably destroyed it when she inherited all of Aunt Jane's papers and the drafts of her unfinished books.'

It occurred to Sarah that if another hand had been involved in writing *Pride and Prejudice*, the countess was the likely culprit.

'Aunt Jane would never have done anything to which Aunt Cassandra objected. Those two adored one another, but Aunt Cassandra was three years older, of course, and she had a small independence bequeathed to her from her fiancé.'

'Her fiancé,' Sarah queried. 'But Cassandra never married.'

'Her fiancé died of fever in Antigua. She dedicated herself to his memory and decided to remain a spinster.'

'Another reason, perhaps, why your Aunt Jane never married,' Sarah said. 'Being so close to her sister, she probably thought that if she did marry, her sister would be hurt. Her marriage might come between them. That says something positive about your Aunt Jane's sensibility and concern for another person's feelings.'

'I never thought of that. You could be right.' As though suddenly realising that she had said more than she intended, Fanny stood and said, 'It's been a pleasure meeting you. I hope your article will do justice to my aunt. Despite her faults, I think she meant well, especially to me.'

Sarah rose from her seat and, while proffering her hand, said, 'I am greatly obliged to you Miss Knight. You have been exceedingly generous with your time. I am a great admirer of your Aunt Jane's works. I believe her reputation will increase as time passes. Be assured, I shall do her justice in my article. I have one more favour to ask. Do you have an address for Miss Anne Sharp?'

'I don't but I expect Papa has. I'll send someone down with it if he has.'

She touched Sarah's hand and then glided gracefully out of the room. Sarah felt glad the interview was over. She had not liked Fanny, whom she thought arrogant and cold-hearted, even malicious. She thought she probably took after her father, a man who, it seemed, had made his wife risk death every year for eleven years with her eleven—or even more—pregnancies. The high mortality risk was well known and great, even for the wealthy and educated. If this was married love, Sarah thought, not for the first time, she wanted none of it.

A footman entered and escorted her to the front door where the gig would be brought to without delay. She spotted Elizabeth with her sketchbook in hand, seated on a little stool in the shade of a tree about a hundred yards away. As she strolled towards her, a maid caught up with her and handed her a slip of paper with Anne Sharp's address on it. She could be reached at Chevet Park, near Wakefield, Yorkshire.

Chapter Eighteen

As Sarah approached, Elizabeth looked up from her work. 'Useful?' she asked.

'Very. Strange and surprisingly revealing.'

Sarah put a hand lightly on her friend's shoulder and, looking over it, studied her drawing. The rough sketch of the house showed its outline and proportions, and Elizabeth had made thumbnail drawings of some details as though the work was more of an aide-mémoire than a finished drawing.

'Do you have enough information for an illustration?'

'Plenty. I'll need a couple of days on it, no more.' She put away her pencils and prepared to leave. 'Where do we go to now?'

'I need to discuss possibilities with you.'

While on their way back to Canterbury, Sarah summarised what she had learned from Fanny Austen. She concluded by saying, 'As a result of today, we have two more people to see, both of whom should be very interesting. Harris Bigg-Wither at Manydown might have a few things to say about the way Jane jilted him. It would have been embarrassing for him if nothing else. As for Anne Sharp, she could turn out to be by far the most useful source of information. If she is prepared to tell us everything she knows about Jane—and we can be sure she knows a great deal—it would put everything else we've been told in perspective. Apparently, she became Jane's closest friend. She will want Jane's side of the story to be told.'

'You said she lives somewhere in Yorkshire.'

'As far as I know she works for a Lady Pilkington as governess for her four daughters. The address I have is Chevet Park, near Wakefield in Yorkshire. I don't know how near Wakefield is to York. It could be miles away.'

She paused and took hold of Elizabeth's arm with her free hand. 'My dear, if we go north, it will be at least two days' journey each way. We could need two days with Anne Sharp. And it might turn out to be for nothing of much value. I'm wondering if it might be a good idea to write to her first and then invite her to come to us in Basingstoke. The magazine will pay her expenses and a fee for her time and contribution to the article.'

'We have nothing to lose by asking. She might even welcome a holiday if she's working as a governess and is entitled to time off.'

'Then that's what I'll do,' Sarah said.

Elizabeth replied, 'So that's the two extra people we need to see.'

'Are you sure you can spare more time?'

'Of course I can. This whole business is a wonderful adventure for me. And you need a companion.'

'I don't know about a companion, but I need you, my dear,' Sarah said lightly. She cracked the whip above the horse's head and it promptly broke into a trot.

They remained silent for a while and sat comfortably in the gig enjoying the day and the countryside.

Eventually, Sarah said, 'You know, my love, I feel that I'm going to get a lot more than just an article on Jane Austen out of it. Somewhere among all this information about her life, there is a play waiting to be extracted, not necessarily about her, but about the life of a woman writer at the turn of the century. It would need to be somewhat Shakespearean in style, I think. Lots of characters in short scenes with a subplot of some kind to provide comic relief.'

'That sounds fascinating.'

Sarah continued pensively, 'It would be a challenge, but if I could get a popular actress to play the lead, I'm sure Drury Lane would put it on. No one expects long runs these days. Audiences want variety and short seasons. Most new plays are given only a few performances. If the staging isn't too expensive and the management can get the right actress for the lead, they will take a risk with it. And if my new play is a success, I'll be in a stronger position when actors like Mr Kean throw a tantrum. Drury Lane seats over three thousand. A full house, even for a couple of nights, is worth a small fortune to a playwright. If the play runs for as many as three nights, I will receive the profits from the final performance.'

'Then, dearest, we should do everything we can to help you write a wonderful play.'

'Then I'll write to Anne Sharp as soon as we get to Canterbury. I'll give the circulating library in Basingstoke as our address and make that town our base. On our list to see, then, are Mary Austen, who "wants to put the record straight", at Steventon; Cassandra, the sister, at Chawton, although she's likely to be uncommunicative or very protective of Jane's reputation, so I should leave her to last; and the sailor, Frank Austen at Portsmouth. Are you happy with that?'

'Completely,' Elizabeth replied.

'Then it's decided. We could go from Canterbury to Portsmouth, but if we try to go direct, it will be a miserable cross-country journey and will take for ever. I suppose we could go from here to Folkestone and get a sea passage to Portsmouth, but that might easier said than done. A better plan, I think is to return to London, pack everything we are likely to need for at least a week in Basingstoke, then take a fast service direct to Portsmouth—a morning's journey. Then we'll see Francis Austen if we can, and then go from there to Basingstoke, another short and easy journey. Within a day or two, perhaps longer, we should receive a reply from Anne Sharp. In any case, we'll need several days in Basingstoke to visit Steventon, Chawton and Manydown. Are you happy with all that?'

'Of course, dearest. There'll be plenty for me to draw and paint.'

'That's what I hoped you would say. When we finally get back to London, you can decide which of your drawings to have engraved and used as illustrations for my article.'

Chapter Nineteen

Post-Captain Francis Austen, RN had very little to say to Sarah when she visited him at his Portsmouth lodging. What he did say, however, confirmed her suspicion of the veracity of the statements in Henry Austen's memorial to his sister.

He welcomed Sarah gruffly, but courteously, very much the no-nonsense naval officer. He expressed his pleasure that she was taking so much trouble to learn of the realities of his sister's life before publishing anything about her.

'She was a determined and ambitious woman,' he said. 'Very talented. She deserves the recognition she craved. Writing as much as she did was not easy for her. She had household duties and was often unwell. But she persisted, snatching a half hour here and a half hour there. She rarely had more than an hour a day to spend on her novels.'

When Sarah quoted what Henry Austen had written about her attitude to her work, the Captain scoffed loudly. 'What rubbish!' he exclaimed. 'What the devil was the man thinking? He must have been ill when he wrote that nonsense about her.'

'You are quite sure he was mistaken? He was very involved in assisting Jane to sell her books.'

'My dear woman, I have letters from Jane totally contradicting him. Out of the horse's mouth so to speak. She desperately wanted praise for her writing and to make as much money as she could from it. And as for not wanting her name to be associated with the books, she wrote to me before the publication of *Emma* saying she was tired of lying about her authorship—all the family and friends knew she was the author of the first three books anyway so what was the point? She intended putting her name to *Emma*.'

'But she didn't.'

'Apparently not. I can't explain it. You will have to ask Henry or Cassandra. My sisters were as thick as thieves.'

Sarah said, 'If Mr Henry Austen can be so wrong about Jane's attitude to her work or the income she enjoyed from it, I suppose it is possible that there are other statements in the memorial that are less than completely correct.'

'I've never read it, so I cannot say.' Frank Austen took out his pipe and began to fill it with tobacco, first asking for Sarah's permission. Abrupt and outspoken though he was, his manners were impeccable.

Changing the subject, Sarah asked, 'Have you any views, sir, on why Jane withdrew from the engagement to Mr Bigg-Wither?'

Frank Austen roared with laughter. 'You'll know if you meet him. Harmless fellow, but no girl's knight in shining armour. Plenty of money though. Manydown is a splendid property.' He puffed contentedly for a few moments, then queried, 'Are you a single woman, Miss Kedron?'

'Yes.'

'And have no doubt been offered marriage by many handsome men of good family and adequate fortune.'

Sarah smiled. 'A few.'

'But you have declined them all. Why?'

'I value my independence more than anything,' she said. 'I make my own living as a writer for the theatre. If I marry, as the law stands, I lose control of everything I own, including the copyrights in my plays. My husband, if I had one, would be able to prevent me from publishing my work, and could insist on censoring everything I wrote that he did not like or with which he did not agree.'

'There is the answer to your question. Jane also valued her independence. Her life until recently was a constant struggle to make ends meet. The temptation to marry and at least solve her financial problems must have been great. It is well that you, and not a man, are writing an account of my sister's life. You will be able to get under her skin as no man possibly could.'

He stood. 'Now, madam, I must ask you to excuse me. I have an appointment I must keep. And I am always on time. It has been a pleasure meeting you, and I wish you success with your critical and dramatic endeavours.'

Sarah stood and offered her hand. 'And I, sir, am most obliged to you. You have given me a great deal to think about. Your sister's reputation is in good hands; I promise you.' However, she wished he had had more time to spare. She believed him to be a straight-forward man, who had been an affectionate and understanding brother to Jane, but the interview was over. Captain Francis Austen escorted Sarah to the door.

The meeting had been brief but enlightening, and well worth the journey, but the return to Basingstoke would have to wait until the morrow since it was now too late in the day to take a coach.

Overnight, Sarah had to decide whether the next meeting should be with Cassandra Austen or the Reverend James' wife, Mary. She was very aware of how important it was at this stage of the investigation not to make a mistake. She suspected that the Austen close family network was as efficient as any governments' spy network. Every question she asked and every answer given would be widely and promptly reported.

Chapter Twenty

They arrived in London from Portsmouth in the early evening. After spending the night at their respective homes, they departed for Basingstoke immediately after breakfast the next morning. As soon as they had settled in the coach, Sarah said, 'I suggest we stay in Basingstoke for as long as it serves our needs. We may be able to get a larger room at that pleasant hotel we stayed at last time. I feel guilty that I have rushed your painting and sketching, my dear. Let's make this a time for you, and I'll fit in around what you want to do. We can go for picnics if the weather is fine. Take our time riding around the district, getting to know it, the feel of it.'

'You don't have to do that,' Elizabeth told her. 'I've been very content following you around, and I've done some work.'

Sarah smiled. 'I would like you to do more. The Basingstoke district is Jane Austen country. Steventon, where she spent the first twenty or so years of her life, is just an hour's ride away and so is Chawton where she spent most of her last years. Manydown, where she almost became the mistress, is only about three miles away at Wootton St Lawrence. I would love to have a series of your drawings of all these houses and gardens to illustrate the article.'

'Then I shall consider this a commission,' Elizabeth replied. 'I can think of nothing I would rather do.'

'Then that's agreed,' Sarah replied. 'You are now the official illustrator for my article! I will have my father put you on the payroll. We've been constantly on the move for almost a fortnight. And I'm still being selfish. I may need several days in one place so that I can sort all the notes and jottings I've made. And we have to include time for Anne Sharp in our plans; that is, if she comes.'

Elizabeth happily agreed. 'Then I think it's a lovely idea. Thank you, dearest. You're very thoughtful.'

'That's settled then. As soon as we arrive in Basingstoke, I will write to Mary Austen at Steventon asking for a time to visit her. We know she wants to talk. She's told us so. I will also write to Harris Bigg-Wither at Manydown. He may agree to see us out of curiosity. And we'll try to see Cassandra Austen at Chawton, but it might be difficult to persuade her to talk to us. We know that Henry, who was closer to Jane than anyone in the family except Cassandra, has written a seriously misleading piece about her, for whatever reason we may never discover. But if he and Cassandra are in this piece of deception together, then she is unlikely to welcome us.'

Their journey to Basingstoke was fast and comfortable on turnpikes all the way. At the White Hart Inn, they secured a larger room, which was spacious enough to use as a bed-sitting room. Had it not been, Sarah had intended finding a suitable lodging elsewhere in the town.

While Sarah spent the rest of that day writing letters, Elizabeth shopped in the town for the things they would be likely to need. She also borrowed a few novels from the circulating library.

Harris Bigg-Wither replied promptly to Sarah's letter with an invitation to afternoon tea at Manydown. Sarah's problem would be how to approach the all-important subject of his proposal of marriage, Jane's acceptance and then her withdrawal less than twenty-four hours later. At the very least, Sarah thought, the man would feel embarrassed, even humiliated, and possibly still very angry. His proposal had been made in 1802 while the Austen's were living in Bath and were just visiting Manydown. Sarah decided that she would adjust her approach to the subject of the proposal according to the kind of man Bigg-Wither was.

Much to her relief, he turned out to be the kind of man she hoped he would be. Jovial, courteous, very much the Lord of the Manor which he had become a few years before, leading a country squire's life full of hunting, shooting and fishing with all the usual rural pursuits and social occasions. He himself broached the subject of his proposal as soon as the maid had cleared away the tea things.

He had a bad stammer, but he managed to circumvent it by using different words and phrases. 'The place where I live' became 'my home' or 'here.'

'You will want to know about my pro ... posal of m ... marriage to Jane,' he said, leaning forward confidentially. 'As far as I know, mine was the only one she ever had, so I sup ... pose it is im ... portant.'

'If it is not insensitive of me to ask,' Sarah said.

'Not really. I was annoyed at the time, and Jane, Cas ... sandra and their mother, left in a hurry in some con ... fusion after Jane told them what she'd done. Mrs Austen was furious with Jane. Mind you, that would have been nothing new. They did not get on. Cas ... sandra was Mrs Austen's favourite and Jane knew this. Not unnaturally, she resented it.'

Bigg-Wither now settled back in his high-backed armchair, prepared and perfectly willing to tell his story. Sarah thought it was one he often told, probably to anyone who would listen.

'You have to understand,' he said, continuing to stammer in places, 'the Austen family's situation at the time. The Reverend George Austen had retired, given up his living at Steventon to his son, James, and moved to lodgings in Bath. It was a foolish move and unnecessary. He could have stayed on at Steventon until he became too ill to attend to his duties. I heard, I think from Mary Austen, that when the Reverend Austen suddenly announced to the family that he had decided to retire and hand over the Steventon living to his son, James, Jane fainted with a cry and fell to the floor. Ha! She had to be brought round with Mrs Austen's smel … ling salts. Those salts received a lot of use with her, believe me. Jane just adored Steventon. She'd known no other home. As it was, the family left for Ba … Bath with little income. They even had to sell the rector's library. That would have hurt Jane. There's no doubt that in a word, they were poor. Jane had been writing steadily for several years and had written several short stories and three novels. As far as I know, about three years before they left Steventon, her father offered one of Jane's novels to Mr Cadell, the pub … lisher, but he rejected the work sight unseen. After the move to Bath, her brother Henry offered another of her novels to Benjamin Crosby. He bought the copyright but never published it. Jane was devastated. You see, she had believed that her work would be published without difficulty, and that it would be well-received and earn hundreds of pounds. The family's difficulties would be over thanks to her ability and hard work. As it was, she had achieved nothing. Not only was the family still poor, but worse, she was dependent on them. And now, with her confidence shattered, she was finding it very difficult to write anything.'

'And Jane told you all this?' Sarah said.

'I learned it through our mutual acquaintances. I was just twenty when I offered m … m … well, Jane was five years older, but we had known each other throughout my childhood. From her family's point of view, Jane needed a husband like me whose inheritance would provide not only for her, but for them, and I was very fond of Jane. I believed she would have made an excellent wife for me.'

'Did she want children?'

'I never asked, but I do not think so. That did not matter. I have an abundance of nephews to carry on the family name.'

'You are suggesting,' Sarah said, 'that you offered marriage out of friendship and kindness for her and charity for her family.'

'To a large extent, yes. The Knights provided the living at Steventon, and Jane's brothers, James and Edward, had benefitted. I thought I could do the same for Jane.'

'And she realised that.'

Bigg-Wither replied, 'Oh, yes. And at the time, she thought it was her duty to her family to accept my prop … osal. Her mother liked to talk about her aristocratic connections, and marriage into the Bigg-Wither family would be have been very satisfactory. The Bigg-Wither estate is over four hundred years old.'

'But during the night, Jane changed her mind.'

'Yes. I don't think she slept at all, and she faced painful recriminations when she told her mother. Her explanation would not have been acceptable to Mrs Austen. Jane told me that she had promised herself from a very early age that if she married, it would be for love, not for money or social position. She soon realised that if she married me, she would be breaking that solemn promise to herself. I was hurt and somewhat dissap … pointed but understood her situation. We would never have been happy. I was impetuous to prop … ose, and she meant well by accepting me but realised how unwise it would be. I am grateful to her for her courage and honesty. Two years later, I married, and now have an abund … ance of children to carry on the name.'

'And, I, sir, am most obliged to you for your frankness,' Sarah said. 'You have helped me towards a greater understanding of Jane. And you are a most magnanimous gentleman.'

Bigg-Wither had little more to say and Sarah nothing more she wished to ask. The purpose of the meeting had been fulfilled. She stood and brought it to an end. The outcome was different from what she had expected, but it all made good sense.

Chapter Twenty-one

Two days after their arrival at Basingstoke, a letter arrived from Mary Austen. The speed and positive contents of the letter made it clear to Sarah that the woman was not only willing to talk about her late sister-in-law, she was almost desperate to do so. Sarah began to feel optimistic about the revelations that the meeting might provide. Thinking over all the conversations she had had so far with members of the family, she realised that, although they believed they were presenting a united front with their attitudes to and feelings for the writer, in reality this was far from the case. Everything they revealed about Jane was coloured by their own experience of her, and this differed from one person to another as much as did their individual characters. It occurred to Sarah that Henry's downright lies had little to do with Jane. As a failed banker with nowhere else to go, he had in later life decided to take holy orders. He had not, Sarah thought, had an epiphany on the road to Damascus. His decision had not been that of a man who has had a profound religious experience. It was the decision of a man who, with little chance of obtaining suitable employment for a man of his class, age and education, needed a job. A curacy was the best he could get. Accordingly, he needed to present himself as a man to whom being a good Christian of the Anglican persuasion was important. By stressing his sister's saintly behaviour, which was probably as much a fiction as her novels, he was drawing attention to his own.

The Austen Knights had a different view of Jane. They had not mentioned her piety. Fanny Knight, who had apparently been close to her aunt, had been sufficiently concerned to make clear that Jane was a poor relation and not of the same social level as she and the Austen Knights were.

Captain Frank Austen had nothing in particular that he wanted to present and had, Sarah thought, been totally honest. Bigg-Wither wanted to present himself as a decent man, rich in sensibility in his understanding of Jane's plight, and determined that he should not be thought resentful or even slightly annoyed at being jilted by her.

Sarah felt strangely excited as she rode a hired horse towards the Steventon rectory. She had no idea what Mary Austen's confidences would be, but she was sure they would be a major contribution to her understanding of Mary's late sister-in-law's character.

Mary Austen met her at the front door and made her feel welcome. A maid immediately served tea in the library. And after the usual conversation about the weather and such neutral topics, Mary came to the point.

'It is impossible to understand anything about Jane without taking into account her relationship with Cassandra. I grew up with the family, as did my sister, Martha, and she lives with them now at Chawton. Cassie is three years older than Jane and was as much a mother to her as a sister. Mrs Austen was often ill, and although for several years she entered into the spirit of many of the activities we enjoyed, she became increasingly religious and, I am sorry to say this, neglected Jane badly. Cassandra became her sister's emotional rock. Jane worshipped her. And this fierce love was returned. They became inseparable.'

'You mention the activities you enjoyed with the Austen family as a child,' Sarah said. 'Can you tell me more about them?'

'The most enjoyable were the play readings and the plays we put on in the barn. The family loved the theatre, and Jane even wrote for it, as did my husband. He wrote prologues and epilogues for the plays.'

'How old was Jane when she started writing?' Sarah asked.

'About fourteen, perhaps a little older.'

'And you were close friends.'

'Very. That is, until her cousin, Eliza—the so-called Comtesse de Feuillide—came on to the scene.' The expression on Mary Austen's face darkened. The conversation had reached a turning point. Mary Austen continued, 'Eliza, Mr Austen's sister's child, was married to the French count when she first visited Steventon, that would have been in about 1793. She came for Christmas and to take part in the theatricals. The world was that woman's stage, and she dominated any room she entered.'

'Was her husband with her?'

Mary Austen shook her head. 'No. He stayed behind in France to attend to his estate. Then he was guillotined during The Terror. No one in the family except Eliza's mother ever met him. She had a son by the count, a boy called Hastings after his mother's godfather and benefactor, Warren Hastings. But the boy died young. For a while, Eliza seemed to enjoy being a widow, but then she decided to marry again. Her first choice was my husband. Fortunately, he had the sense to ignore her attempts to seduce him, so she turned to Henry and they married a year or so later and lived in London where Henry later founded a bank. As an only child and William Hasting's godchild, Eliza was never short of funds, so they lived an interesting social life. Eliza took Jane under her wing, became her muse and mentor, I suppose. She was a disturbing influence in the family. Bold, flirtatious, outspoken with extraordinary views on marriage and morality in general. Mrs Austen, my mother-in-law, disliked her and mistrusted her. Jane seemed to idolise her, but I have come to think that Eliza was using her for her own purposes. We often had literary evenings when we would read aloud from books we liked, and Jane was encouraged at these evenings to read her works in progress to us. The Reverend George Austen had a good library and was interested in literature and encouraged her. He had a copy of Mary Wollstonecraft's *A Vindication to the Rights of Women*. It almost became Jane's bible.'

Sarah asked, 'Was Jane religious?'

'Dutiful rather than devout.'

'You say that you believe Eliza Austen was using her for her own purposes. In what way?'

Mary replied, 'She took it upon herself to advise Jane about her writing. No one speaks of it, but Jane's first novel, written when she was about twenty was inspired by her. It is a scandalous story about a titled but poor widow who is determined to marry again for more money and a better social position. To achieve her end, she destroys the marriage of her best friend. She has a daughter, whom she mistreats and who she is determined to marry off to a wealthy old man. When she fails in her attempt to trap her friend's husband, she marries the old man and finds another equally unsuitable man for her daughter.'

Sarah paused to collect her thoughts and then said, 'Did Jane read aloud from this novel?'

'Yes. And when she did, you could hear a pin drop. Then Mrs Austen stood up and said, "We do not want to hear any more of that disgraceful rubbish," and left the room. Jane burst into tears and ran to her bedroom, followed by Cassandra.'

'The poor girl must have been very upset.'

'She was devastated. It was days before she would leave her room. Cassandra took up all her meals. I am not exaggerating when I say that evening changed Jane's life. She became moody and often withdrawn. We rather drifted apart. She only wanted to be with Cassandra.'

'What do you think was the problem with the novel?'

'There were two. The unsuitable subject matter for a novel by a clergyman's daughter especially as the author could be interpreted as being sympathetic to the appalling woman. The novel is epistolary and full of letters written by and to the woman. They are totally convincing. But they are not what you expect a woman novelist of her class to write. It would have been acceptable if written by Henry Fielding or even Samuel Richardson, but a rector's daughter! Dear me, no. And perhaps even more serious, it was obvious that the character was inspired by Eliza. How dare Jane use family members for fictional purposes!'

Sarah said, 'I suppose Jane knew from then on that she would have to self-censor her work and write only what the family would approve.'

Mary nodded. 'Family yes, but mainly in the person of Cassandra.'

'Whom Jane would not want to displease.'

'Yes. And Cassandra is very God-fearing and has strong opinions. She likes going to suitable plays but is disgusted by the personal lives of so many of the players. And there is always Mrs Austen to be considered.'

'Forgive my impertinence in asking this, but are you friendly with Cassandra and Mrs Austen?'

'We make an effort. Jane, I'm afraid, became resentful when James inherited this living and we moved into the rectory after his father retired. Emotionally, this was her home.'

'Captain Austen told me that Jane had difficulty finding time to write because of all the household chores in which she had to share.'

'I'm sure that's true. We drifted apart as we grew older, and I regret this, but it happens in families for all kinds of reasons. But I can tell you that I think it is little short of a miracle that Jane wrote as much as she did and that most of it is so good.'

'Do you have a favourite novel?'

Mary smiled. 'Definitely *Emma*. It has the most depth to it.'

'What became of the novel that caused all the trouble?'

'Probably destroyed. Cassandra has inherited all her papers. Only she knows what is in them. She is very protective not only of the family name, but of Jane's reputation.'

'Did Jane keep a journal?'

'Of that, I have often wondered. However, I would think that she did. Most women of our class do, and most writers do, don't they?'

Sarah laughed. 'I do not, but I am still wondering whether I should.'

The meeting, Sarah thought, was being extraordinarily fruitful. Mary Austen was doing her best to be both interesting and honest. Her views on Eliza and her mother-in-law were especially interesting. A noise from the upper floor disturbed Sarah's thoughts. Aware of the situation in the rectory, she said, 'I know your husband is ill, Mrs Austen, I expect you would like to attend to him. With your permission, I will take my leave. I cannot emphasise enough how valuable your confidences to me are. I shall be totally discreet in how I deal with them in my article. It is the self-censorship aspect that most interests me. This is at the heart of the problems that women writers have, especially those from respectable middle-class families.'

Mary stood, walked towards Sarah and embraced her, tears in her eyes. 'Jane would have so loved to have met you. I believe you would have had so much in common.'

Chapter Twenty-two

A letter arrived from Anne Sharp the next day. Sarah broke the seal and quickly skimmed the contents. 'She is on her way,' she exclaimed, 'but doesn't say when she expects to arrive. She will take whatever coach she can get when she reaches London. Her employer is travelling on the continent with her daughters and her services aren't needed. She says this will be the first holiday she's had for years.'

'That's such good news, dearest,' Elizabeth said. 'She must want to talk to you.'

'I think so, but here,' Sarah tapped the letter, 'she says she'd also like to visit Cassandra Austen and her mother. When Jane was alive, Anne came to Chawton with the Austen Knights. They have a large property there. Cassandra and her mother have one of the cottages on the estate. She also met Cassandra and her mother when they visited Godmersham.'

'Then she may be able to advise you how to approach Cassandra.'

'Indeed, she may.'

Sarah read the letter again, carefully this time, in case she had missed something in her haste. But the letter was short and to the point. Sarah said, 'I'll leave a message with the landlord to give her their best remaining room and whatever she needs in case we are out when she arrives.'

Anne Sharp arrived very late in the evening on one of the night coaches from London to Portsmouth via Basingstoke. Sarah met her guest for the first time the next morning at breakfast in the dining room.

It surprised Sarah to see that Anne Sharp was quite elderly, with iron-grey hair and a rather forbidding expression. When she smiled, however, she revealed the warmth and sensibility of her nature.

She left her table and came forward to greet them. They all shook hands, Sarah introducing Elizabeth as her dearest friend and the artist employed by the magazine to illustrate her articles.

During their breakfast, Anne Sharp revealed a little about her life in Yorkshire, mentioning that she was planning on retiring from her employment. She had been left a small property in Everton, on the outskirts of Liverpool, and hoped to open there a small seminary for girls, perhaps of about twenty of them from fifteen to eighteen years of age. Such an establishment, she hoped, would provide her with an income and a home.

After breakfast, the three women walked to the circulating library where they were lucky to find an unoccupied nook. As soon as coffee had been served, Sarah raised the subject of Jane Austen by asking, 'When did you first meet Jane?'

'It must be about fifteen years ago. Mr Edward Austen had recently moved from Rowling to Godmersham and needed a governess for the oldest child, Fanny-Catherine. Mrs Edward Austen was having a child almost every year, so there were seven children when I arrived in 1804 and nine before my ill health forced me to leave nearly three years later, and two more after I left! Mr Edward's mother brought Jane and Cassandra for a visit not long after I had settled in.'

'And you became friendly then with Jane?'

'Mrs Austen made it obvious from the beginning that she much preferred Cassandra to Jane, almost to the extent of ignoring Jane completely. I can't say I blame her. Jane was often very direct, even rude. It was just one of those unfortunate clashes of temperament. I can't remember hearing of a single incident that caused the rift between them. Mrs Austen just seemed to take against Jane. She behaved the same way to her husband's cousin, The Countess Eliza. I was told she refused to have her in the house.'

Elizabeth asked, 'How did Jane respond to this kind of cold shoulder treatment?'

'I don't think she cared much,' Miss Sharp replied. 'I gather she had never felt close to Mr Edward Austen or, indeed, any of her brothers. When Jane visited Godmersham, she preferred to spend her time with the children, reading to them, playing games. She was very good with them and became particularly attached to my charge, Miss Fanny.'

Sarah considered this and replied, 'I suppose, then, it was natural that as she spent time with the children, she became friendly with you.'

'I don't know about natural. True, we walked the grounds together, but I was just a governess, and she was a relation of the family.'

Elizabeth observed, 'But a poor relation.'

Miss Sharp nodded. 'Yes, there was that. The house had a good library, and I had use of it, so I read whenever I had time. It was inevitable that Jane and I should talk about the books we read.'

Sarah said, 'Did Jane talk about her own writing, and her ambition to become a writer?'

'Not at first. But gradually she began to confide in me. We rarely met; it was largely a friendship by correspondence.'

Sarah believed that if Anne Sharp had kept Jane's letters, they would be an invaluable source of information. She also knew that it would be a gross impertinence if she asked to read them. If Anne thought Sarah should read them, she would have to be the one to raise the subject. Sarah repeated pensively, 'A friendship by correspondence. Yes, I believe Jane was a dedicated letter writer.'

'It was the way we kept in touch. It wasn't until I'd left Godmersham that she confided in me, and then I began to understand her suffering.'

Elizabeth raised her eyebrows. 'Suffering?'

'Mental anguish,' Miss Sharp replied. 'She appreciated that her only chance for independence in her life was to earn sufficient income from her novels. And she accepted that the demands of her family denied her that opportunity. Life had been difficult enough for her at Steventon where they had several servants to do the work, but when her father retired and the Steventon living and rectory passed to James, they moved to lodgings in Bath with a single maid. She had very little time to herself.'

Sarah said, 'That explains why she wrote very little until they moved to Chawton. She just revised existing work.'

'They were difficult times for the family. Desperately short of money. Cassandra had a small income from the bequest her fiancé left her, and Mrs Austen may have had a few pounds a year. Jane, of course, needed money for her writing. Paper is expensive, and most authors pay to have their books published. If they don't sell well, an author can lose more than two hundred pounds. That would have been almost a year's expenditure for three women living in cheap lodgings. Jane did not have that kind of money to risk losing it.'

After adding a little cream to her coffee, Anne Sharp continued, 'After the tragic death of her fiancé, Jane's sister, Cassandra vowed to remain a spinster. I sometimes think Jane did the same out of love for Cassandra. She thought it would be cruel to marry when they were so close. If either took a husband, it could not but help come between them.' She paused to sip coffee, then said, 'I'm sure you've read that piece by Henry Austen in which he tries to make out that Jane was a saint.'

Sarah nodded.

With a hint of bitterness, Miss Sharp continued, 'Well, he's immortalising the wrong woman. Please, do not take this wrongly, I liked Jane, but Cassandra is the saint. She is a deeply pious woman, rather narrow in her views and perhaps intolerant, but a thoroughly good woman whose life is dedicated to looking after other people. Her religion, her faith as a Christian of the Church of England, is the most important thing in her life. She really ought to be a bishop's wife. She is, was, hugely protective of Jane and puts up with her mother's real and imagined illnesses without complaint. She manages the household. When Elizabeth—Edward's wife—died ten years since, Cassandra immediately travelled to Godmersham to take over the household and stayed for a year. And, of course, when Jane was ill, which she was for at least two years on and off, it was Cassandra who nursed her.'

Elizabeth asked, 'How did Cassandra behave towards you?'

'I was the governess. She behaved as she should have behaved. I have no complaints.'

Sarah said, 'You said in your letter that you would like to visit her at Chawton.'

'If it is possible. It would be discourteous for me to be in the district without at least calling and leaving a card.'

Realising immediately that this might provide her with the opportunity for a favourable audience with Cassandra Austen, Sarah said, 'Then I suggest I order a gig to take you there. We can resume our conversation later.'

Anne Sharp said, 'You are most kind. Thank you.'

The women left the library and walked back to the hotel. There, Sarah ordered a gig to take Anne Sharp to Chawton and arranged to meet her for dinner.

Chapter Twenty-three

Before Anne Sharp returned from Chawton early that evening, Sarah and Elizabeth met in the dining room and Sarah ordered wine. She felt like celebrating that, at last, they were beginning to understand the very complex nature of the late Jane Austen. Before they had each taken more than a sip of wine, Anne Sharp joined them at their table.

'I hope your visit was pleasant,' Sarah said.

'Yes and no,' Anne replied. 'Miss Austen expressed her pleasure—and surprise, I might add— in seeing me, but she made me welcome.'

'I am relieved,' Sarah said.

Miss Sharp continued, 'She is devastated by her loss and is still in the deepest mourning. There were times when I wondered whether she will ever recover.'

Elizabeth asked, 'Did she tell you much about Jane's last illness?'

'A little. It was prolonged with periods of what seemed like recovery but then she would have a relapse. They have no knowledge of the actual condition other than that it seemed to be a type of wasting disease. Jane was in considerable pain. I had the impression that much though they regretted her death, they accepted it for the best. At the end, they took lodgings in Winchester to be nearer her doctor, but he explained that without the possibility of a cure, an early death was all they could hope for.' She paused to sip some wine that had been discreetly poured, and then said, 'I felt I had to explain what I was doing here.'

Sarah agreed that was appropriate. 'Of course.'

'Miss Austen knows you are writing about Jane. Her brother has told her. He is the local curate but doesn't live with them. There are just three of them in the cottage; mother and daughter and Martha Lloyd. I understand that she is an old friend of the family.'

Sarah nodded. 'Yes. Her sister, Mary, is married to James Austen, the rector of Steventon. Did you mention that we hope to talk to Cassandra?'

'I did. Out of courtesy she will receive you, but I think it most unlikely she will want to talk about

Jane. I get a decided impression that the family are putting on a united front about her. It's almost as if her life was an embarrassment to the family, and they are trying to present it as something very different from what it actually was.'

'I think that often happens in families.' Sarah smiled. 'Black sheep change colour on the way to the cemetery.'

A servant came to take their food order. As soon as she'd left, Sarah said, 'I feel that I am beginning to know Jane a little, but there is much about her life that I do not understand.'

'Such as?' Anne Sharp asked.

'For a start, what happened to the first novel she wrote? I can't help thinking that it is very significant in her life.'

Miss Sharp replied, 'I cannot say much about her earlier work as I was not acquainted with the family, but I understand that Jane was very influenced by her cousin who insisted on being called Countess Eliza. She was much older and had a reputation for leading a rackety social life in London. Her first husband remained in France for most of their marriage.'

'Was she a bad influence on Jane?' Elizabeth asked.

'That rather depends on one's point of view. Young though Jane was when she came under the influence of the woman, she was mature enough, I am sure, to be aware of the rumours surrounding

Eliza's paternity, but—and this is the crux of the matter for Jane—Eliza was confident, well educated and could be very charming. She loved being the centre of attention and knew how to get it. Had she not married the Frenchman and received substantial support from her godfather, I am sure she would have gone on the stage, and, no doubt, become a successful courtesan. She fascinated Jane, but deep down, I think Jane did not really approve of her. If the novel to which you refer is the early epistolary work from which Jane allowed me to read a few short extracts, then it has either been destroyed or is among Jane's papers, all of which are now in the possession of Cassandra. From the few extracts that Jane sent to me, I formed the impression that the novel is somewhat ambiguous in its tone. It is quite difficult to know whether the author approves of her main character or not. There is no authorial voice, just letters from the main characters. Jane told me that shortly after writing it, she read chapters aloud to the family, but then her mother very forcibly put a stop to it. Her mother could not understand how her daughter, not yet twenty and with little experience of the world outside Steventon village, could write about an adventuress, apparently with such tolerance of her behaviour.'

Elizabeth asked, 'How did Jane feel when she was criticised for writing it?'

'It was something of a miracle that Jane did not give up writing. She gave up writing plays because of her mother's attitude to the theatre and, in particular, to the players.'

'So she did write plays?' Sarah asked.

'As a young girl, yes, a few. And very short novels. Mostly comedies. Social satires. Parodies of what she read. Even as a girl she thought that the behaviour of adults was ridiculous. She made fair copies of everything she wrote as a child and had them bound in three volumes. It was as if she was pretending to be a professional writer. They are labelled Volume One, Two and Three.'

Elizabeth smiled. 'Have you read them?'

'Yes. Jane showed them to me when I visited Chawton. For a young girl of her background—she was only about fifteen when she wrote them—they are extraordinary. Not at all the kind of thing one would expect a clergyman's daughter to write. They are an attack on the stupidity of so much social behaviour. I remember one vividly. It's called *The Visit,* and it's about some minor aristocrats visiting relatives. They behave as though they are attending a royal banquet but are being served tripe and onions and similar poor people's food. At the end, various couples who have only just met, decide to marry. It's ridiculous but a very biting satire.'

Elizabeth said, 'I would love to read Jane's juvenilia. It must tell us a lot about her.'

'There's no doubt of that. I expect Cassandra has it all locked away somewhere. It's a shame. Jane wouldn't have gone to such trouble copying and binding the work if she had wanted it to remain hidden.'

'Perhaps there are other plays that only Cassandra knows about,' Sarah suggested.

'It's possible. I tried to encourage her to write plays. Her dialogue is wonderful. But she knew that her mother, and, to a lesser extent, Cassandra would condemn her if she did. They had a not uncommon attitude to the theatre. They enjoyed it but disapproved greatly of the morals and private lives of the players.'

With a laugh, Sarah said, 'I should tell you that I was an actress for five years.'

Anne Sharp blushed. 'Forgive me, I didn't mean to imply ...'

'I know you didn't. And the way some players behave is far from acceptable in polite society. I suppose Cassandra was concerned that if Jane became a playwright, especially a successful one, people would assume she too had what, for want of a better expression, I'll call theatrical morals.'

Anne Sharp nodded vigorously. 'Precisely. And remember the Austens were a clerical family. Jane's father was a rector, and two of her brothers are in holy orders. And there is the social aspect to be considered. They valued their place in respectable rural society. They ranked as lower gentry.'

'And Cassandra held the power to prevent Jane from writing plays.'

'I think so. For most of her life, certainly, though in her last year or so, she worked on dramatising Samuel Richardson's novel, *Sir Charles Grandison*. It was one of her favourite books. I do not know this for certain, but I think she knew she was dying and wanted to write something that was important to her, in spite of Cassandra's opinion. Jane wanted to leave something for the theatre.'

Sarah sighed. 'This is so sad. If Jane Austen had written a successful play, even just adapted *Pride and Prejudice*—it's nearly all great dialogue—it would have provided an income, even if it had just been published as a closet drama, to be read aloud but not acted on a stage. Do you have any evidence that Cassandra prevented Jane from writing for the theatre?'

'Only what Jane told me. Cassandra once sent her a diatribe against the theatre by a well-known agitator. A clergyman, of course.'

Elizabeth said, 'You are suggesting quite strongly that Cassandra was very controlling of Jane.'

'Their relationship is difficult to understand. Jane adored her sister. She went out of her way to please her. Even when by doing so, she was sacrificing her own needs. She hated being apart from

Cassandra. They shared a room for most of Jane's life and shared every thought. Cassandra's good opinion of Jane was desperately important to her. It is strange that we allow people we love to control us. But we do. Think of so many married women. They love their husbands but are enslaved by them.'

Sarah stared through the window. Even though night was falling, hurrying pedestrians, carriages of all kinds, passenger coaches and carriers' wagons filled the busy street.

A servant approached and refilled their glasses with wine. Anne Sharp was not used to alcohol, and it loosened her tongue. Elizabeth also felt the effects of the wine and asked to be excused.

As Elizabeth left the table, Sarah said to Anne Sharp, 'Do you think that if Cassandra had not been around, Jane would have written different books?'

'I've often wondered. Throughout her life, Jane was experimenting. She stayed within the milieu that she knew. She would not have strayed from that. But in style, all her novels are different. I sometimes think her novels would have been more explicitly radical if she had felt freer to express herself. She would have taken more risks.'

'Been a reformer like Mrs Edgeworth, perhaps?'

'Perhaps. But Sarah … May I call you Sarah?'

'Please do. I shall call you Anne.'

'We must never forget that the novels Jane wrote are the novels of a woman who is trying hard to be what she is not. It is that tension in them that gives them something of their quality. I believe the novels will last for ever and become increasingly popular in time. I'm afraid I'm not explaining it very well.'

'Not at all. You are most insightful.' Sarah sipped her wine and then, as she put down the glass, said, 'You believe that in her writing, Jane was trying to be in fiction what she was not allowed to be in life. What do you mean by that?'

'Her novels can be enjoyed as light reading. Cheerful positive books. It's hard to find tragedy in them. There's not a lot of weeping. Not a lot of death in childbirth. Not a lot about women desperate to have lives of their own, financial independence, freedom to be themselves, have their own opinions. There is almost nothing explicit about the world beyond the little world that Jane would have known. She was writing during one of the momentous periods of our history. The French Revolution, the loss of the American colonies, the Napoleonic Wars, to say nothing of the incredible social changes taking place. Yet there is scarcely a word about any of them. But what there is, somewhere in every book she wrote, is something presenting the plight of women like me. I am but one of thousands of governesses or teaching drabs. Too plain to seduce a potential husband. Too poor to purchase one, but, if the opportunity presented itself, willing to marry a man for financial security or social position, even though I might find his appearance or behaviour distasteful.

'You are a fortunate one, Sarah. You have a rare talent that can produce an income. As has your beautiful friend. You have the courage—or perhaps the support of an understanding family—to strike out for yourself. Jane could not. She was trapped by poverty, religion and class. Her novels are about that, but they do not upset readers who do not want to be upset. Husbands are happy for their wives to read Jane Austen because they don't know what the books are really about.'

Sarah could hardly believe her good fortune in having met Anne. She felt as if she'd struck a rich seam of gold. 'Can we discover Jane's own views on many issues from a close reading of the books?'

'That is a dangerous practice. Do you want your audiences to think that the opinions of your characters are your opinions?'

Sarah retorted, 'Most certainly not.'

'The same applies to Jane's writing. If we wish to know what she feels and believes, we need to read her letters.'

'Did she keep a journal?' Sarah asked.

Miss Sharp replied, 'I don't know. She never referred to one. Most women like her keep them, of course. And I assume that all writers do. If she did keep one, it will be in Cassandra's keeping along with her other papers, her letters, and drafts of unpublished novels. Who knows what else she left? Cassandra is her executor and firmly in charge of what the world will be allowed to know about my beloved Jane. And that is why I am willing to talk to you. The real Jane Austen was not a contented woman spending her life arranging the flowers for the church, reading uplifting sermons, living a life of piety, relieved to have survived the birthing of ten or more children and determined that her daughters shall be like her. The real Jane Austen was angry at the plight of the poor, of middle-class women, of women in general, but she had to hide her anger.' Anne Sharp took out a handkerchief and dabbed her eyes.

Elizabeth returned to the table and presented a head and shoulders pencil sketch of the elderly governess. 'May I give you this, Miss Sharp?' she said, handing her the drawing, 'as a memento of our meeting?'

Anne took it and gazed at it. 'My dear, that is so sweet of you. That's very kind. It will be the second treasure I have been honoured with today. Miss Austen gave me a lock of my dearest Jane's hair.' Overcome with emotion, she rose from the table and hurried out of the room.

Chapter Twenty-four

The next morning, Sarah and Elizabeth arrived at the dining room shortly before Anne Sharp.

'I hope you will forgive me,' she said as she joined them, 'but I must return to Wakefield today. It will be two days before I get there.'

'I was hoping,' Sarah said, 'that you would stay with me in London for a few days.'

'You are most kind, but I am expected back. I have enquired with the inn keeper, and he assures me there is an available seat in the London coach.'

'I'll organise it for you,' Sarah said. 'It has been so good of you to travel all this way and you have provided much upon which I shall ponder. When I write my article about Jane Austen, I will be greatly indebted to you.' Anticipating this situation, she handed Anne an envelope. 'This is a very small token of my appreciation, dear Anne, and an attempt to ensure that you are in no way out of pocket. I am deeply obliged to you.'

She had given considerable thought to how much she should give the governess. Too little would be disgraceful. Too much could have the appearance of charity and be almost as equally insulting. She had settled on ten pounds, of which she thought about half would cover the travelling costs. The coach would have cost six shillings for every forty miles, plus a shilling for the driver and another shilling for the guard, a total of eight shillings. She estimated the round trip at four hundred and fifty miles, a total cost of just under five pounds. The extra five would be an acceptable gift, she thought.

Anne hesitated in taking the envelope but realised that to decline it would be ungrateful.

Conversation remained general during breakfast. After which, Sarah and Elizabeth took their leave to drive to Chawton. Sarah promised to stay in touch with Anne and send her a copy of her article about Jane for her comments before it was published.

Sarah said nothing during the hour's journey to Chawton, rehearsing in her mind what she would say to Cassandra Austen and what she would ask. Anne

Sharp had not been optimistic about the meeting but had not wanted to discuss it.

When they reached Chawton, Elizabeth said, 'I'll stay with the gig and sketch the cottage, and also the village if I have time.'

Sarah nodded. Then, feeling very apprehensive, she got down from the gig and walked along the short path to the front door of the cottage. After knocking, nothing happened for several long moments, then the door opened sharply revealing a short, middle-aged woman dressed from head to toe in deep black. Sarah opened her mouth to state her business, but the woman, who she soon realised was Cassandra, spoke before she could utter a single word.

'I know who you are, and I have nothing to say to you. I have nothing to share with the Grub Street gutter press whose hacks take delight in spreading wicked gossip about innocent people.'

'Please, Miss Austen, I …'

'Everything you need to know about my beloved sister is in her novels. Read them with care and respect.'

'Of course, and I have, but …'

'We are entitled to our privacy. Why do you think you have any right to spread rumours and lies about my family? What business is our family life to the world outside our homes? What is to be gained by your speculation about this and that event?'

'Readers of your sister's …'

'The books are all there is for them. If it is not enough, that is too bad. The rest is for the family and God.' She moved forward, her eyes glaring at Sarah, daring her to interrupt. 'I have lost a treasure, such a sister, such a friend as never can have been surpassed. She was the sun of my life, the gilder of every pleasure, the soother of every sorrow. I had not a thought concealed from her, and it is as though I have lost a part of myself. Now, I beg of you; leave us in peace and go with God.' And she closed the door in Sarah's face.

Too shocked to move, Sarah stood quietly at the door for several moments. Then, unconsciously trembling in shock, dismay and confusion, she turned and walked slowly back to the gig.

Seeing the expression on Sarah's face, Elizabeth realised that the meeting had not gone well. Saying nothing, she handed Sarah up into the gig. As soon as she was seated, Sarah took her friend's hands in hers. 'It was so wrong of me to call on her,' she said. 'My instincts told me at the beginning to have respect for Cassandra's mourning. We should always obey our instincts, dear heart. Let us go.'

Elizabeth picked up the reins and, without talking, they began their journey back to Basingstoke.

When they arrived at the inn, Sarah said, 'I don't feel like the journey to London today. Would you mind if we stay here another night? We could have an early supper and retire early.'

'Whatever you wish, dearest. I can understand how you must feel. You go on in. I'll see to the groom.'

Sarah got down from the gig and walked into the inn. Elizabeth returned the gig to the stables. Their adventure, she thought, was now over.

Chapter Twenty-five

Later that evening, when they had been in bed for at least an hour, Elizabeth, aware that Sarah was restless, said quietly, 'Would you like me to send down for a hot drink, or a brandy, dearest? I know you can't sleep.'

'Jane's life is going around and round in my head. I need some kind of completion.'

'Perhaps if you told me what you know.'

'A lot of it is guesswork. Filling in the blanks left by the people to whom we have talked. And everything is so subjective. I have no hard evidence for any of it. So little of it has been in Jane's words. If only I had access to her journal—if she kept one—or even some of her letters, I would be nearer the truth of her life.'

'You would be nearer her truth, but would it be the real truth? How would you know that her own account of her life was the truth? It would be coloured by her own character, desires and disappointments, wouldn't it?'

Sarah conceded, 'You are right, of course. Very well. Cuddle up, and I'll begin.'

They made themselves comfortable and Sarah began her summing up.

'This will be the gist of my article. Jane Austen was one of eight children of the Reverend George Austen and his wife, Cassandra. The six boys and two girls were all born in the rectory at Steventon. The living was not a particularly rich one, but there was a farm attached, and the family were able to live well off the land. This is where we will insert your sketch. To add to the income, Jane's father, who provided most of her education, had a small boarding school for boys at the rectory. He was an educated man, well read, with a good personal library of his own. His wife, who was also reasonably well educated, took to her bed after her eighth child and left the running of the household to her eldest girl, Cassandra.

'In spite of, or perhaps because of the house being full of boys, Jane tended to be a lonely child who took refuge from all the noise and boisterous behaviour in her father's library. For emotional support, she relied wholly on Cassandra whom she adored and who reciprocated her love. Mrs Austen had little affection for Jane. She much preferred the always helpful and well-behaved older sister.

'Jane was capable of tantrums and acts of rebellion. She could be sullen and impertinent. She discovered at an early age that one had to fight for what one wanted. A significant example of this occurred when she was about eight years old. Her parents decided to send Cassandra, who was twelve, to a girls' boarding school. When Jane realised that she was going to be left behind and parted from her adored sister, she threw such a tantrum that her parents gave way and she was allowed to accompany Cassandra. Throughout her life she hated being apart from her, and if they were ever apart, she would write daily to her, sometimes twice or more.

'Jane's childhood was far from being unhappy, however. There were plenty of good times. Jane especially enjoyed the family theatricals. The older boys had turned a barn into a small theatre and the whole family put on plays, especially at Christmas time. It was these that gave Jane her love of the theatre. And it was because of them that she came under the influence of her cousin, Eliza, the Countess de Feuillide.

'Eliza, who was at least ten years older than Jane, was the daughter of her father's sister, Philadelphia. Born in India, she had been educated in France, and married a French count. She lived in London with her mother while her husband managed his estate in France. Eliza was confident, clever, charming, and often outrageous in her social behaviour and opinions. She loved the theatre and visited Steventon to take part in the theatricals. Realising, perhaps, that Jane needed the companionship of a woman other than her sister, she took her young cousin under her wing and became her mentor.

'It was about then that Jane began to write. Throughout her late childhood, she filled notebooks with plays, sketches, miniature novels. Many of them were parodies of plays and novels she had read. In many of them, she made wicked fun of what she saw as the absurd social behaviour and ridiculous etiquette of the social class of which she was a member. She was especially aware of the obsession of young women with finding a suitable husband—one who had a fortune or a better social position. Precocious and amusing, she was at first encouraged. Only later did her parents, in particular her mother, realise how dangerous her writing could become.

'This situation became obvious when Jane was about twenty. She wrote a novel, epistolary in style, about a society widow who is determined to marry another wealthy, high-born man even if this involves breaking up his existing marriage. At the same time, she is trying to force her daughter into a marriage with a much older man whom she loathes.

'It was customary for Jane to read her writing aloud to the assembled family. When they realised what the new novel was about, her mother and sister were horrified. Not only was the subject matter inappropriate for a rector's daughter, but there was even the possibility that the character of the adventuress was inspired by Countess Eliza. Jane was told to destroy the work, and never to write such a story again. Their dilemma was that they did not want to stop Jane from writing, especially as it was possible her books could contribute to the family's income, but she had to be prevented from writing the wrong kind of book and putting in her stories characters drawn from life.

'Apart from exercising a degree of self-censorship, Jane was not permitted to publish under her own name. Her father took it upon himself to try to find a publisher for her next book, which would be "By a Lady."

'Shortly after this event, her father retired from the Steventon living, which passed to his eldest son, James. The family, now in much reduced circumstances, moved to lodgings in Bath and later Southampton. When Jane was told of this move, she went into shock and fainted. It was as though her secure life had come to an end. She realised that she had nothing to look forward to except a marriage to a man she probably would not even like, let alone love, assuming any man would want a plain woman without a dowry. Or she would have to settle for the lonely life of a governess who would be little more than a slightly superior servant.

'Determined not to marry without love, she became even more reliant on her writing ability. Her first sale—for ten pounds—was not encouraging. Her next, was far more so. It earned her almost two hundred pounds.

'She was aware that although women writers were few, some were successful. Maria Edgeworth, Fanny Burney, Ann Radcliffe were all earning substantial incomes. Jane's problem was that she needed to write novels that would not only sell but would not cause her family social embarrassment. Her mother was especially anxious that people would not think that Jane wrote for money.

'The years in Bath and Southampton were fraught for Jane. She found it very difficult to work. Money was tight. They had only one maid, so she had to help with the household chores which interfered with her writing. She was earning very little. Cassandra became engaged to be married but her fiancé died of a fever. Fortunately, he left her a useful legacy. Eliza's count had been guillotined during the Terror. Anxious to be married for the social benefits and respectability that marriage brought, she soon set her cap at James—Jane's eldest brother—but he rejected her. She then approached another brother, Henry, who married her. They were not short of money as he became a banker for a time, and she had her own fortune. Jane, Cassandra, her mother and a family friend, Martha Lloyd, struggled on.

'Then their situation changed. Edward, another brother, had been favoured by the wealthy Knight family. He had now inherited their estates, one of which was at Chawton, not far from Steventon. He offered them a cottage on the estate. At this time, Jane also received a proposal of marriage from a childhood friend. At first, still not earning much from her writing, she accepted, but withdrew the next day not wanting to risk losing her independence and betray her principle of marrying only for love. Instead, she threw herself into her writing, and at Chawton, she experienced the most productive period of her life. Tragically she became ill, possibly because of over-work and emotional stress. She wrote steadily until the day of her death at the age of forty-one.

'It was not until after her death that Cassandra, who became her executor, permitted her novels to be published under her name. Her brother, Henry, whose bank had failed and who had taken holy orders, published an obituary in which he maintained that Jane had wanted neither fame nor fortune from her novels and that she had insisted that she not be named the author of the novels until after her death.

'Throughout her life, Jane wrote nothing that could embarrass her family in any way if her authorship became known. She restricted her work to novels about the social class with which she was familiar and the concerns of young women.'

Elizabeth sighed. 'Is that it? Not much of a life, really, was it? There doesn't seem to have been any emotional highs. No great love affairs. No children. No exciting travels. No thunderous applause. Just fear of poverty and the need to write.'

Sarah Kedron closed her eyes, knowing that she would not even attempt to write a play about Jane Austen. Instead, she would write one about a woman who did not censor herself, who proudly identified herself as the author of her works, who married for love a man who encouraged her radical ideas and her rejection of absurd and pointless social conventions. She would make her mark not only as an author but also as an individual.

Relieved at having been able to put her thoughts into order, she began to breathe softly and evenly.

Elizabeth gently extricated herself from her friend's embrace, and they slept. The search for Jane Austen had been both interesting and enjoyable. She was far from sure that they had found their quarry, or that anyone could. Too much was hidden or lost and would probably remain so.

Chapter Twenty-six

On their arrival in London the next day, Sarah and Elizabeth parted to go to their own homes, Elizabeth to pursue the new commission to paint a family portrait, and Sarah to write out the summary of her findings and have a messenger deliver it to the Reverend James Stanier Clarke at Carlton House.

She did not have to wait long for a response. Within the hour, a royal courier delivered a brief note from the Reverend Clarke that invited her to Carlton House where, at two o'clock in the following afternoon, she would take tea with Lady Hertford. Sarah did not hesitate in accepting the invitation. Lady Hertford, who although rumoured to be approaching the end of her tenure as the Prince

Regent's mistress, was sufficiently influential at court and in the Tory faction to be a person whose acquaintance was worth cultivating.

Accordingly, dressed in her finest silk dress and wearing the most extravagant hat from her small but impressive collection, Sarah took her father's carriage to Carlton House in time for the appointment.

The Reverend Clarke welcomed her warmly and led her to an exquisitely decorated and furnished drawing room where Lady Hertford sat at a table, reading. He announced, 'Miss Sarah Kedron, ma'am.'

Sarah bowed and dropped a small but awkward curtsey. Lady Hertford smiled and rose serenely from her chair. 'Come and sit at the table, my dear. Tea will be here shortly.'

As Sarah walked to the table already laid with a tea service, Lady Hertford said, 'My spies tell me you have a new play coming at Drury Lane.'

'All being well, Your Ladyship, yes.'

'We are very keen on amateur theatricals at Ragley Hall, our place in Warwickshire. Perhaps you would be able to join us there some time.'

'I should be delighted to.'

As she resumed her seat, Lady Hertford indicated that Sarah should also sit. Further conversation was delayed until a footman, who seemed to have materialised out of thin air, had poured the tea, and another footman, presumably from the same hiding place, had offered milk, and yet a third presented sugar. It was all rather ridiculous, Sarah thought, but she was happy to play her part in what she knew to be a charade designed to show off wealth and social importance. She also wondered what it would be like to be a house guest at Ragley Hall, the seat of the Hertford family for at least a hundred years.

Lady Hertford said, 'I have read your report with great interest, Miss Kedron. I imagine there must have been many questions you would have liked to ask, but you considered them to be impertinent or insensitive.'

Sarah replied, 'That is especially true when I was interviewing members of the family.'

'Indeed. I am most obliged to you for going to so much trouble to satisfy my curiosity. The quest must have taken a great deal of your time.'

'It was a fascinating experience for me. I was accompanied by an artist friend who made sketches of the people we met and the places we visited.' Sarah smiled. 'It is I who should be obliged to you, Lady Hertford. Without your interest, I would never have undertaken the investigation. I enjoyed it so much that I am considering repeating the experience with a different subject.'

'Really? How interesting. Do you have anyone in mind?'

'Mary Wollstonecraft.'

'Good Gracious! A more different woman from Jane Austen it would be difficult to find. Although she died while still in her early thirties, there are many people still living who will have known her. Mr William Godwin, whom she married, is an acquaintance. I shall be pleased to provide you with a letter of introduction to him. And to his clever daughter, of course. Mary Shelley, although she never knew her mother; tragically, Mrs Mary Wollstonecraft passed away within a few days after her birth.'

Lady Hertford sipped her tea, and then asked, 'But tell me. Did your investigation provide an answer to the quest? Can we be assured that Jane Austen penned all the novels that bear her name? Your report carefully ignores this question.'

'That is deliberate for the reason that I was not able to find any conclusive evidence that she did or did not. Although Miss Austen was entitled to claim the authorship of *Pride and Prejudice,* I believe she may have received enthusiastic encouragement and probably extensive advice from her cousin, the late Eliza Hancock, the former Comtesse de Feuillide, and later, the wife of Jane Austen's brother, Mr Henry Austen.'

'Ah, the legendary Comtesse de Feuillide. In what way would she have influenced the novelist?'

Sarah was slightly surprised at the innuendo expressed in Lady Hertford's tone, so she chose her words carefully. 'Oh, I believe Eliza or Countess

Eliza, as she insisted on being called, became involved in the development of characters, plot ideas, and may even have suggested lines of dialogue.'

'From what I have heard about the Countess,' Lady Hertford replied, 'I can believe she would have had plenty to say about the story. Is there anything else?'

'Well, Your Ladyship, at the time when Miss Austen was writing the novel, Eliza, who by that time had married Henry Austen, was seeing her frequently and, of course, corresponding. Although I must stress that I personally do not suspect that her involvement would have been more than superficial. I believe Jane Austen to have been a woman of the greatest integrity. I cannot imagine for one minute that she would have applied her name to another person's work.'

'Is it not possible that the help she received would explain why she insisted on anonymity?' Lady Hertford said.

'It is possible, Your Ladyship,' Sarah conceded.

'Well, I suppose we will never know the whole truth. You are aware of course, that the librarian here, the Reverend Clarke corresponded with both Miss Austen and her publisher. It was his account to the Prince Regent that first aroused the doubts about the authorship. The Prince is most concerned as he had specifically requested that the book *Emma* carry his personal endorsement.'

Sarah replied, 'I am sure the truth is concealed among the documents bequeathed by Jane to her sister, Cassandra. These will contain, apart from letters, early drafts of novels, her contracts with publishers and, although I have no proof of this, even Jane's journal.'

'Really? You do not refer to a journal in your report,' Lady Hertford said with surprise.

'That is because no one to whom I spoke had ever seen or been told about one. The only person who thought she might have kept one was her niece's former governess, Miss Anne Sharp, who appears to have been her most intimate confidante.'

'And what is your opinion? Do you think it likely that Miss Austen kept a journal?'

'I consider it most unlikely that she did not. Most educated young women keep one. For a woman who is determined to be a successful writer, not to do so would be extraordinary, and if she kept one, it will be in Cassandra Austen's keeping. But it would not be at all surprising if she destroys it along with any correspondence that might offend or hurt the people to whom the writing refers. I fear that Miss Cassandra Austen will see it as her Christian duty not only to safeguard their feelings but also her sister's integrity and reputation.'

Lady Hertford replied, 'Then unless we hire a burglar with a very large sack to visit Miss Cassandra Austen's residence in Chawton, we must wait patiently for developments. Perhaps with an encouraging request from the Prince Regent, Miss Cassandra might allow an expurgated version of the journal to be published.'

'I think that unlikely, Your Ladyship,' Sarah said. 'And I honestly doubt whether such a version would tell us anymore than we already know.'

'Very true. But let us now talk of other things.' Lady Hertford smiled, and Sarah thought that she was such a pleasant woman it was difficult to imagine her associating intimately with the Prince Regent. 'When would it be convenient for you to visit Ragley Hall?' Lady Hertford asked enthusiastically. 'I would appreciate it so much if you could give the actors advice.' Her face brightened as she had an idea. 'We could put on one of your plays! Now that would be a splendid thing to do. The cast would be so appreciative. When can you come?'

'I'd love to be involved,' Sarah replied, 'but may I let you know when I shall be free to leave London? My new play will go into rehearsal soon, and I should be available at rehearsals until after the first night. That will probably be towards the middle of next month.'

'That's settled then. Just let me have a week's notice. And don't worry about transport. I'll send a carriage for you. It's been such a pleasure meeting you, Miss Kedron. Thank you again for doing so much to satisfy my curiosity.'

Lady Hertford rang a small bell. Within the blink of an eye, a footman appeared to escort Sarah to her carriage.

While returning to Portman Place, Sarah pondered the consequences of having agreed to the Reverend James Stanier Clarke's request and how close she had been to refusing his invitation! But new doors were being opened to her. She wondered what she would find behind them. Experience had taught her that one development in her life inevitably led to another. The more she welcomed new experiences, the richer her life became.

Publisher's Note

If you enjoyed this book, we would be very grateful if you could write a review and publish it at your point of purchase.

Your review, even a brief one, will help other readers to decide whether or not they will enjoy this work.

Do you want to be notified of new releases?

If so, please **sign up to the AIA Publishing email list**.

You'll find the sign-up button on the right-hand side under the photo at www.aiapublishing.com. Of course, your information will never be shared, and the publisher won't inundate you with emails, just let you know of new releases.

Other books by Ken Methold

The Missing Baronet

If you liked the character of Sarah Kedron, you'll enjoy *The Missing Baronet* in which the wife of Sir Charles Browning asks Sarah to find out what has happened to her husband who has disappeared without trace. Sarah Kedron and James Brewster, the editor of her father's weekly periodical, investigate the disappearance. Their search for the truth takes them from the high society of Regency England to its shady underbelly. Firmly established in the social, political and economic conditions of the time, *The Missing Baronet* is an enthralling read.

What readers are saying about *The Missing Baronet*:

'A meticulously researched period piece, bringing together colourful characters, conflicting aspirations and a tricky mystery so solve.'.
B.J.Haydon

'This is an absorbing thriller with a complex plot and well-drawn characters. There are just a few tantalising leads to reveal the surprise ending. Overall this is an extremely good read.' R. Ross

The Missing Baronet is available as an ebook and paperback from Amazon, and as a paperback from The Book Depository and by order through all good bookshops.